No Turning Back

Book 3, The Liliana Series

by

Neva Squires-Rodriguez

Vanilla Heart Publishing

No Turning Back
Book 3, The Liliana Series
by Neva Squires-Rodriguez

Copyright 2015 Neva Squires-Rodriguez

Published by: Vanilla Heart Publishing
www.VanillaHeartPublishing.com
10121 Evergreen Way, 25-156
Everett, WA 98204 USA

ISBN-13: 978-069244-61-57   ISBN-10: 069244615X

10 9 8 7 6 5 4 3 2 1 First Edition

First Printing, May 2015
Printed in the United States of America

No Turning Back

Book 3, The Liliana Series

by

Neva Squires-Rodriguez

Table of Contents

Dedication and Acknowledgements

More Great Books by Neva Squires-Rodriguez

Author Bio, Photo, and Contact Info

Dedication

This book is dedicated to my husband, Cecilio. I thank you for being my best friend. We've come a long way and I thank you for the changes that you've made in your life to make this work.

Acknowledgements

First and foremost, I would like to thank God for always giving me direction in my life.

To my mother, Delia Squires, I thank you for proofreading my work and giving me ideas on what works and what doesn't. I truly appreciate that. To my father Thomas Squires, thank you for buying so many copies of my book. You're the greatest!

To my author bestie, Tamara Philip, thank you for constantly promoting my books and God bless you in your upcoming marriage to Chris, wishing you both many happy years together.

To my friends at Vanilla Heart Publishing, Chelle Cordero, Charmaine Gordon and Lauren Shiro, I don't know what I'd do without you. Chelle, you constantly promote me over social media and I greatly appreciate all you do. Lauren, who helped me greatly by thinking up the title of this book, you are top notch!

To my writing group, Weekend Writing Warriors, you are a support team like no other. I greatly appreciate spending my Sundays with you.

Finally to Kimberlee Williams my publisher, thank you. Besides writing, it blows my mind that you are caring enough to reach out to me in weather emergencies to check and see if we are ok here in Illinois. There is no other quite like you and I love working with you!

Chapter One

I sat completely still for what felt like hours. I could hear Antonio's watch ticking slowly as he sat before me waiting for a response. What was I supposed to say? He had just finished telling me that he was the one who shot my mother. What was I supposed to say to him or to anyone? I felt as if I was sitting in a room full of strangers. Even worse, I suddenly felt like I didn't know who I was. I wanted to get up and storm out of the room, to get as far away from everyone as I possibly could, but I couldn't move. I felt like my body had frozen, as did everything else around me.

"Liliana say something." I heard Elena say.

I sluggishly turned and gazed at Elena and the rest of the family without saying a word. Not a tear fell from my eyes as I sat staring at them, however my eyelids blinked, notifying me that I was in fact awake. I turned very slowly and looked up at Antonio. His eyes appeared both apologetic and eager, as he waited for my response without saying a word. The truth was I didn't know what my response would be. I needed direction that no one in the room was trustworthy enough to give me.

I silently closed my eyes and lowered my head folding my hands in my lap and asked for direction from the only being I felt credible enough to guide me. I felt the hairs on my arms stand up as I felt the burn from everyone in the room watching me. I needed direction and at this point I didn't care who was watching me. I did the only thing that I could think of doing and I prayed silently as the entire room full of people, all of which were Antonio's family watched me. I felt Elena put her hand on my shoulder, but I moved it away, remaining seated next to her.

When I opened my eyes, everyone stood before me frozen in time and waiting for my response. I felt surprised with myself and the fact that my eyes were dry even though my heart felt like it had broken in half within my chest. Antonio and I stared deep into each other's eyes, me suddenly remembering every detail from the night that he shot and killed my mother. Gun shots echoed in my mind as one of the maids entered the room to see if anyone needed anything. Sensing the thinness in the air, she immediately went back to the kitchen. I shook my head to bring myself back to reality as I sat before Antonio and cleared my throat.

"I have to see him." I said silently.

"What?" Antonio asked, not hearing the words as they left my mouth.

"I have to see my father." I said louder. "El Jefe."

A huge commotion immediately went through the room. Antonio's cousins instantly came to his side and began talking to him very quickly in Spanish. One began to yell directly at him, surprise showed on Antonio's face as he attempted to stop himself from standing and ripping his cousin's head off. I could tell how badly everyone in the room took what I had just said, but I didn't care. Antonio tried to be calm, but within seconds, he was yelling back and all of the other cousins stood up to pull the two of them apart. Blanca came back downstairs and stood in the room with a distressed expression upon her face. She held her hand to her chest but said nothing as everyone watched the commotion fill the room as if it was a gigantic wave.

I sat before the entire family as they argued. If I tried to understand what they were talking about, I'm sure that I could have. Instead my mind was elsewhere. I couldn't help but to replay the night that my mother died in my mind, the events repeating over and over. In some ways, I wanted to know what Antonio's family was saying. I wanted to see how much of my story they already knew, but at the same time, what I really wanted to do was to talk to my father.

I couldn't help thinking of the mysterious man that I watched from afar as he sat down with Antonio in our backyard. The man that had eyed my children and smiled. Did he want to be a part of my life? Did he want to be a part of their lives? Why did he choose now to make his presence known?

I wasn't sure why I wanted to talk to this man, the man that everyone hated so badly. I questioned myself as I sat observing the intensity of the room. The only thing that I could think of was my father because I was certain that he was the only one who had the answers for all of the questions that I had. I began to wonder if he remembered my mother and what information he could give me about her. Surely a man like him had to have had at least a hundred relationships after her. How was he expected to remember her?

I glanced around the room and watched the people I knew as my family fight and couldn't help feeling angry and hurt as I stared intently at each one of them. I felt betrayed by everyone. How could they have known about what Antonio had done and expect me to be ok with it? How could they live with themselves, knowing what Antonio and the rest of his family did for a living? As I sat watching them I realized that I suddenly felt like I had betrayed my mother. How could I have lain down with the man that killed her? So what if I didn't know. Why didn't I see the signs? Those eyes, that I had sworn so long ago that I would never forget, I didn't even recognize until now.

A lone tear fell from my left eye as I sat as still as a stone sculpture and watched as everyone else in the room became lost in their own anger. When the room finally fell quiet and Antonio's cousins stepped away, Antonio took my hands in his and looked me in the eyes. I shook my head as I gazed up at him. I looked away momentarily, glancing around the room and noticing that everyone's attention was focused on the two of us. The burn from their stare was intense and I felt heat burning into me as I quietly examined my surroundings. Blanca seemed to be full of regret as she watched us and Elena no sooner stood up, than she fell into Miguel's arms, quietly sobbing as if it would modify the situation.

"Did you hear what I just said?" He asked quietly. "I killed your mother."

The lone tear finally fell from my chin as Antonio sat studying my expression. I couldn't believe that he had just repeated his statement to me. He said the words slowly, as if that would make a difference. He said them in a way that made me feel like a child and suddenly I realized that before this moment I had been like a child to him. While we made love like husband and wife, he had always felt the need to protect me, neither of us realizing that it was himself that I needed protection from. I had been under his control and at his disposal and it suddenly made me angry. I felt my face begin to steam, my ears turn red and finally my heart turn to stone as I reached up and pushed the hair back from my face, allowing me to look him directly in the eye as I spoke.

"I heard you." I responded angrily. "Did you hear me? I want to see my father."

Antonio stepped back from me as if I had just slapped him in the face. My words hit him hard. I knew how powerful my response was to him and I knew that I had just disrespected him in front of his family. I couldn't begin to imagine what everyone must be thinking, but from their expressions, I had a pretty good idea.

Every last one of them hated my father. I didn't have to know what was going on, to see this. At this point I wasn't sure if they were more shocked by my response or with me wanting to see him. I questioned myself as to whether or not they all hated me now, knowing who my father was. I glanced quickly around the room, but then refocused my attention on Antonio. At this point he was my only concern; I would deal with the rest of them when I was good and ready.

Chapter Two

Our gaze was intense. I could tell that Antonio was trying to contain his anger. He literally appeared as if he was about to explode. Antonio cleared his throat and broke our gaze about a minute later, turning around to contemplate the reaction of his family. I knew that he was wondering if they had caught my act of disobedience. He observed their expressions to determine what move to make next, but when he saw the blank expression on some of their faces, his gaze returned to me. I sat tall in my seat, I wasn't about to let him break me.

"Maybe we can arrange something when we come back from Chicago." Antonio finally replied.

I shook my head. I knew that he had no idea how serious I was and I was determined to make him understand it.

"Lily, we can't miss this trip, it's a requirement." Antonio said convincingly. "The whole family is going."

"A requirement for you." I said sternly.

Antonio glanced around the room for approval, before looking back at me.

"The tickets are non-refundable." He said under his breath.

"Then you go." I replied, as I smiled coyly. "I don't want to be around you or any member of your family anytime soon."

"Are you kidding me?" Antonio responded. "Lily, I'm not leaving you by yourself."

"Then leave me with my father." I replied. "Or leave me at the house, the maids are there, we have security. I'll be fine."

"Liliana," Antonio cut in, "Are you hearing yourself right now?"

I nodded at him as I looked up at him and he continued to babble on. He was trying to convince me that I was making a bad decision. I knew that I very well might be making the wrong decision, but it was my decision and my place to decide that. His rambling made my head begin to hurt; I finally cut him off mid-sentence.

"Antonio, I'm not going with you." I said, shrugging my shoulders.

I knew he had no idea how serious I was, but I was determined to show him. I didn't look away. I felt his eyes burn into my own like fire, but I looked through him, telling myself that my mother would be proud of me, for my sudden show of strength.

Elena gasped and the entire room fell silent. Everyone focused their attention on the two of us, even the older children of Antonio's cousins and Elena's two older daughters, who were seated playing card games at a table across the room. I could see Elena shaking her head from the corner of my eye, trying to get me to change my mind, but her wishes were of no importance to me.

"That's not going to happen." Antonio said. "I'm not leaving you here."

"You don't have a choice." I immediately responded.

I heard Roberta gasp and saw her turn away, without knowing where to turn to; she immediately turned back, refocusing her attention on us. I didn't care what she thought either. How dare he, insist that I stay here with the rest of them. How could he even imagine that this was something I would be willing to do?

Internally I was scared, but I had to become my own person now. I needed this; I needed to know my father. I told myself that this was what it would take if I was ever going to figure out anything about myself and who I was. Antonio stared at me for what felt like several minutes, as if this would make me change my mind. I finally shook my head and looked around the room, focusing my attention on each family member individually.

Blanca's eyes were full of sorrow. Her husband stood across the room without making an attempt to console or to say anything to her. Elena leaned against Miguel, as if without his support, she would fall over. Miguel's face was stone cold as he examined Antonio's expression from across the room. When she noticed me focus my attention on her, Elena put her hand to her chest, as if my words hurt her. I couldn't take it. In my opinion they were all hypocrites. I forced myself to stand up and began to walk toward the door, still feeling as cold as stone.

"What about the boys?" Elena said loudly, as I walked away from them.

No Turning Back

I stood completely still for a moment before spinning around and shooting a glare at her that told her this was not the time to question me.

"I need a break." I replied. "The world has come to the conclusion that I should know how to handle multiple devastations that are thrown my way. Call me a bad mother if you want, but I am going to sit this one out. I am going to leave the kids in Antonio's hands because he is their father and he can ask the family for help if need be because it is obvious to me that everyone here is willing to help him or to cover up any secrets that he may have."

I turned back to walk away, but before taking a step further, I looked back at Elena, deep into her tearful eyes.

"I'm not a little girl anymore and I need to figure out what is important in my life." I said.

"Liliana!" Antonio said forcefully, standing up and coming to my side. "I'm not allowing this. I have to put my foot down."

I laughed out loud, without recognizing what it was that was coming from within me. I glanced around the room as more laughter came from within me. It got to the point, where I was so confused with the sound, that it made me laugh harder and harder. My eyes began to water and I reached up and wiped my tears away, forcing myself to stop abruptly and to everyone else's horror my voice came out in one that was not my own.

"You don't get it Antonio." I said. "You don't have a choice any more when it comes to my life. No one does, except me!"

With that I turned and walked out of the room. As I started up the stairs I heard footsteps run out into the hallway below me. I froze in the middle of the stairway, without turning back, knowing that it was Antonio that stood at the base of the stairs watching me.

"Where are you going?" Antonio cried out. "We need to talk about this."

"I'm going to take a shower." I said without turning back to him. "I need to cool down."

With that I started up the stairs, ignoring the commotion that I had just created on the floor below me. I went to the room that Antonio and I always stayed in and closed the door behind me. I leaned back on it with my hands at my sides the moment I was inside. I leaned on it as if it would protect me from my life. I felt like my heart was going at least a hundred beats per minute. I was winded and my body trembled with anxiety.

For a moment I wasn't sure what to do. I stood against the door until my heartbeat slowed down and my breathing became normal. I was surprised that I hadn't started crying and wiped my eyes with the back of my hand, just to be sure that my body wasn't deceiving me. I saw our suitcases on the floor by the foot of our bed and walked over to it, my hands shaking lightly as I fumbled with the zipper. I opened my suitcase, took my clothes out and went to take a warm shower in an attempt to cool my nerves.

The next morning I woke up to loud yelling, followed my doors slamming closed and Blanca's stiletto high heels tapping down the hallway. *Still*? I thought to myself. I heard her inflict rage upon everyone who crossed her path as she walked down the hall and toward my room. Two of the maids apologized as Blanca yelled at them about various things being out of place. Just when I heard her heels reach my doorway, I heard Antonio call out and tell her to go downstairs and eat breakfast. I heard her pause outside of my doorway without saying a word. She touched the doorknob without turning it. I knew Antonio was smart enough to know that it was in his best interest to keep her away from me. After several seconds, I heard her turn and start down the stairway. Antonio exhaled a sigh of relief.

I knew that he had tried to keep her away from me all night. The night before I remembered hearing Antonio fighting with her outside of the doorway. She was livid at the thought that I wasn't going to Chicago with Antonio and the rest of the family and even upon the advice of Antonio and his father she continued to make her fury known by going on about her outrage until the wee hours of the morning.

I shook my head as I heard Antonio confront her and usher her down the stairs. The fighting must have gone on all night. My head still ached from listening to them. I had fallen asleep just after I heard Antonio tell her and the rest of the family to back off and to give him space to make his own decision. To them his response was unacceptable and I was clearly out of my mind. I remembered how last night I heard tires screeching as they pulled away and assumed that it was his cousins leaving the house.

"What?" I heard Antonio scream from downstairs moments before a door slammed shut and commotion broke out, breaking me from my thoughts.

I stretched my arms out and held each of my feet up one at a time, stretching out my toes in doing so. I was determined to stay in bed as long as possible. I quickly buried my head in my pillow as if that would protect my eardrums from the racket Blanca was causing on the first floor. It sounded as though everyone had grown tired of her complaining, allowing her to be argumentative with herself. Before long, the noise simmered down low enough, so low that I felt myself falling right back to sleep. I stared at the wall without moving, trying to relax and let my eyelids wrap themselves around my eyeballs. I asked myself for serenity as I felt my eyelids flutter open to the sound of a sudden outburst from Blanca.

I kicked the sheets from on top of me without moving from the bed. Last night, I had fallen asleep with the vision of Antonio sitting in Miguel's study with the door locked, his head rested against his hands. I knew that he had been worried about what the rest of the family thought and was affected by what had happened between us. At this point, I imagined that no one was concerned about my feelings and my distress having learned that Antonio was the one who killed my mother. I shook the thoughts from my mind as sunlight bounced off of the mirrors and hit my eyes, as if in an attempt to make me realize that it was morning.

I sighed as I opened my eyes wider and looked around the room. From the position of the sun in the sky, I could tell that it was not even seven o'clock in the morning. I hated that no one in else in Antonio's family slept past eight o'clock. They were up having coffee before the first signs of daylight showed in the windows. A normal family would still be sleeping, unless they had to go to work. Our family had the majority of their business done each day by lunch time. Antonio and his family were awake before the first bird started chirping and I didn't understand how any of them could function.

I reluctantly raised my head to the top of my pillow in order to peer around the room. I felt highly irritated that I had been woken up and threw my pillow across the bed in disgust. It didn't feel like I had slept for an hour. My eyes were puffy and watered from sleep deprivation as I wiped the tired tears from my eyes. I stretched out as I felt the warmth of the sun hit my legs and ever so slowly rolled onto my right side. I knew that I needed to hurry and get downstairs if I wanted to say goodbye to the twins.

I glanced at the other side of the bed, realizing that Antonio hadn't slept there, groaning as I forced myself to get out of bed and to walk across the room. Despite my legs cramping up as I walked, I told myself that I had to do it, regardless of the fact that I didn't want to see anybody aside from the boys. I didn't really want Antonio to take the boys to Chicago. I knew in my heart that it would kill me to be without them, but at the same time I felt like I couldn't go on for them without figuring out who I was.

I paused and glanced at myself in the mirror. I felt so incredibly lost, hurt and betrayed that I felt like I didn't even know who the face was that stared back at me. I knew that if the boys stayed in Colombia with me, they would prevent me from getting to know my father the way that I wanted to. Besides this, I wanted them to be able to say that they had been to Chicago at some point of their life. I didn't know if they'd ever have this opportunity again. There was no telling what the future would hold at this point.

I could feel my stomach grumbling uncontrollably. The only thing that I felt like I knew for sure was that I needed to eat. The baby changed positions, as if to point out how impatient it was with me. I stood up straight, my stomach cramping up as I noticed that our suitcases were gone. I had to stop myself from racing downstairs to yell at someone and remind them that I wasn't going anywhere. I was sure that Elena had moved the suitcases not wanting to admit to that I was really was not planning on leaving with her and the rest of the family. I was sure that none of them thought that I had it in me to disobey Antonio and was sure that not one of them was convinced that I would actually stay behind.

I smirked to myself as I noticed an outfit laid out for me on a chair, an outfit that anyone in their right mind, would know that I could no longer fit into. I shook my head, thinking to myself that Elena should know better. I put my hand to my face and let out a long sigh. If I tried to put on the outfit I would look like a clown. I sat debating to myself whether or not I should call someone to ask for a different outfit or if I should walk downstairs the way that I was. I thought of the horrified expressions that everyone would have on their faces if I walked down the stairs without fixing myself up and smiled. I imagined what they would think about me coming down without my hair combed or any makeup on. That would make their day. That would give them something to talk about for hours on the plane ride to Chicago.

I shrugged and laughed to myself as I stood up straight at the side of my bed and walked out of the room without changing out of my pajamas or even running a comb through my hair. I glanced back at the room as I made my way down the hallway. This was it, there was no turning back. I slowly walked down the stairs, hesitating briefly before entering the dining room, where everyone was seated. I smiled awkwardly as I walked in and sat down in an empty chair without saying anything to anyone. I could feel everyone stop what they were doing and turn their attention to me in disbelief. I lowered my shoulders and held my head straight as I tried my best not to look directly at anyone. Yes, I felt uncomfortable, but for some reason I felt like it was all worth it.

My hair was already frizzing up from the heat. I could feel the loose stands as they rose, sticking up as I sat completely still with my hands folded around the table while I waited to be served my breakfast. I didn't even bother to put my bra on before going downstairs and felt somewhat uncomfortable as I sat before them in that respect alone. I looked worse than the day that I had given birth to the twins, but I didn't care.

"Loca." I heard one of Antonio's cousins whisper to her husband.

I nodded my head as if I was in agreement and continued to stare straight ahead and out of a window overlooking the backyard. Antonio turned to his cousin's wife just as she let out a quiet giggle and she immediately stopped, covering her mouth with her hand, as if to hide it. She immediately sat up straight in her seat and pretended as if nothing happened, leaning forward and quietly taking a bite of her food. The room suddenly became so quiet that the only noise we heard were the birds as they sang from the trees surrounding the house. Antonio glared in my direction without saying a word, immediately making me feel uncomfortable. I sat up straight in my chair in spite of the fact that I could feel my face turn red. I wasn't embarrassed with myself, I just was uncomfortable with everyone focusing in on me and I was determined not to let anyone know that I felt that way.

I knew that Antonio knew how badly I was trying to make him upset and turned his attention to his breakfast, quickly shoving a piece of toast into his mouth and rapidly chewing it. The rest of his family stared at him for a while, before reluctantly doing the same. They wanted a battle; I could see it in their expressions. I shook my head, quickly brushing down my hair down with my hands, when I felt everyone's attention had been taken off of me. One of the maids came out of the kitchen and Antonio glanced at me, as if to order her to bring me out my food. She left momentarily as if she understood him and quickly returned with a tray to serve me.

I thanked her under my breath and sat up straight in my chair, pulling the sides of my robe closed over my chest and leaning forward to eat my food. I sat before everyone at the table as if nothing had happened, quietly reaching over and taking a sip of my orange juice. Antonio stared at me intensely as I sat trying my hardest to enjoy my breakfast. The more I ignored him, the more furious I knew that he would become. That didn't stop me and I kept eating my food as if he didn't exist. I ate as if no one else was at the table with me.

"Liliana, what are you doing?" Antonio finally asked.

I glanced up at him. Antonio looked horrible, he obviously hadn't slept. His hand was pressed against the side of his face as he sat studying me with circles under his eyes. Elena glanced at me and then at him, raising her eyebrows, as if to show me how worried she was about his appearance. Antonio's face looked greasier than his hair did. In spite of how frustrated he looked, he sat across the table from me in a freshly ironed polo shirt and blue jeans. His chrome plated Fossil watch sparkled as it clung around his left wrist.

I let our eyes meet momentarily before looking back down at my food. His eyes seemed to pierce through me as he waited for an answer. I felt a chill go through my body, but was determined not to let his expression bother me. I raised my eyebrows without looking up. I knew that he would know that I was acknowledging him, as would everyone else. I also knew that he wouldn't like this reply and it was soon obvious to me that everyone else at the table would know that as well. The table grew quiet as everyone focused their attention back on me as they waited to see what I would say. From the corner of my eye I could tell that Blanca was sucking all of her breath in as if it would prevent her from exploding. I focused my attention on her momentarily before glancing away.

It killed me to know that everyone had known that Antonio killed my mother. How was everyone okay with it and expecting the two of us to continue on with our lives as if nothing had happened? How did they expect me to be willing to accept what happened as if it was just an accident? Antonio

29

could have killed me that night, did they know that he had pointed the gun at me, not knowing that he would end up one day marrying me. I wondered why it was that no one had ever realized who I was or what he did when I first come to Colombia. Why put me to work in a house where I was sure to one day meet the man who killed my mother.

Did they really not know? Would they have done more to prevent us from having a relationship? Would they have done more to insure that Elena and I didn't become as close friends as we had. I just didn't get any of it. What purpose did God have in allowing the two of us to meet? Surely he must have had a plan. Was it a good one, I wondered as I sat staring blankly across the table.

I briefly glanced around the table at everyone, letting my gaze meet each of theirs momentarily, while I tried to figure out what their excuses were. Maybe they had known and forgotten. Maybe they hadn't known at all. Antonio and I met by chance and quickly fell in love. It was possible that no one would have wanted to tell him, or to remind him of his past. He didn't realize that I was his past. I sighed out loud and thought of Elena. There was that long period of time that I lived with Elena; surely someone had figured it out. Was that why Blanca tried so hard to sidetrack our relationship. Had she always known who I was?

I couldn't help but shed a tear as I sat before the entire family in confusion. Surely I must have looked just as confused as I felt. All the while I couldn't help questioning myself on how many people he killed and if he was really done. I was positive that if it hadn't been my mother that he killed, I would have never have found out about what it was that he did for a living. How could I be so stupid? I was so trusting that it disgusted me. I gazed up at Antonio, studying his expression, turning away after he seemed to focus in on my thoughts.

I glanced at Blanca as if to question her on our whole horrible situation. My eyebrow arched slightly as I stared at her and my lip quivered slightly. I noticed her nervous expression as she stared back at me. She knew, I thought to myself. She knew about everything the entire time. My gaze turned to one of accusation and she glanced up at me, as if trying to determine whether or not to say anything to me. Antonio Salvador sat next to her, studying her reaction. He glanced across the table at Antonio and quickly put his arm around his wife as if he meant to keep her quiet. Did he think that would work, I wondered.

I was surprised moments later, when it did. Blanca's shoulders sunk down, as if melting into her knees and she hunched over in her chair. The expression on her face showed defeat and guilt. Antonio Salvador looked away, but did not retract his arm from her. I raised my eyebrows unintentionally as I focused on her, slowly chewing my food as I studied her reaction.

Her short died brown curls seemed to freeze upon her oval shaped head as did the rest of her face, while she gripped her fork, with what appeared to be all the force that she had in her. Her hand shook slightly from the pressure. She glanced over at Antonio, for help, he disregarded her, continuing his examination of me, and I felt his gaze penetrate me as he waited for an answer. He raised his eyebrows at me when our eyes met, and I quickly looked away refocusing my attention on his mother. I didn't say a word as I watched her. I wasn't ready to give anyone the satisfaction of my conversation. Instead of turning and replying to him, I looked down at my food and quickly stuffed a fork piled high with egg into my mouth and proceeded to chew as if everyone else at the table was nonexistent.

31

No Turning Back

My simple reaction was not meant to prove a point or create a commotion, but I knew that it would. Was it wrong for me to instigate an argument? I didn't think so. Not after the news that I had received the night before. Miguel cleared his throat and glanced over at Antonio to see his reaction. I could hear Elena exhale as she waited for Antonio to explode. Rather than to say anything or make anyone at the table happy, I looked at my food as I dug my fork into my eggs for another bite. I wasn't necessarily doing it to make anyone mad, but more so because my own temper was building up. I was in just as much shock with my reaction as anyone else at the table.

Antonio began to tap his fork against the table as if he was trying to control himself. Elena grabbed Miguel's hand and he held onto hers for a while, as if knowing that she was scared of what Antonio's reaction would be, before dropping it and picking up his coffee to take another sip after he noticed me watching the two of them. Antonio's tapping got louder and stronger as he sat across from me. While he tapped, the rest of the room seemed to grow quieter. No one knew what to say and Elena looked like she was afraid to move.

Antonio finally stopped and focused all of his attention on me, not looking away from me as his glare penetrated me deeper than the mornings light. Instead of saying anything he let out a nervous laugh as he watched me. I could see Miguel put down his fork as if he was preparing himself to stand up and jump between us if he needed to. None of this bothered me, not Antonio's reaction or the reaction of anyone else at the table. No one was going to tell me when to talk and when not to anymore. No one was going to persuade me to live a life that was not my own. I proceeded to chew my food with anger as I attempted to make it appear as if I didn't have a care in the world. I could tell my reaction was beginning to scare Antonio, but in spite of this he still chose to confront me.

Chapter Three

"Are you kidding me right now?" He shot across the table in a low voice.

Elena quickly jumped up. She motioned for the nannies to gather the kids and take them out of the room. The twins had already begun crying, it was obvious that they felt the tension in the room. They motioned to Elena with open arms as the nannies carried them past her and Antonio sat across from me gritting his teeth. Elena jumped up and followed them out of the room, talking quietly to one of the nanny's as if she was giving her instructions. Antonio looked down at the table, as if asking it to help him control his temper. I knew that he felt disrespected, but I didn't care. Elena came back into the room, breathing heavily as she sat down at the table. She leaned her head on Miguel's shoulder, watching in anticipation for Antonio's reaction.

I rolled my eyes; it was obvious that everyone at the table was more concerned with Antonio's reaction than with my own. I shook it off and stared at my food, reminding myself that I had my own reasons to be upset. My ears began to burn, to the point that they itched from the burn. I inhaled and exhaled slowly in order to calm myself down. I continued to sit unbothered, chewing my food, with my frizzy hair suspended over my head as Antonio's family watched Antonio in horror.

No Turning Back

"The plane is leaving in two hours." Antonio shouted suddenly, slamming his fist down on the table.

I continued to eat my food without saying a word. I concentrated on the texture of the eggs as I felt rage burning within me. I glanced over to my side after what felt like several seconds, to see Elena sucking her cheeks together as if she was holding her breath. The color seemed to have flushed from her face and she literally appeared as if she would faint at any moment. I knew that she knew what was coming, as did everyone else at the table, the only thing was that they had no idea on what to expect from me.

"Dios lo que he hecho yo para merecer esto?" Antonio said as he stood at his side of the table, obviously trying to control his anger by running his fingers through his hair and tugging at the ends.

Shaking his head, Antonio walked out of the room. I could see everyone at the table turn and glance at each other but Antonio gave them no time for comments, he returned immediately with an expression that made it seem as if he was trying to make the statement that he thought he was in the wrong house. I continued to eat my breakfast without showing any concern. This only made Elena more worried and Antonio more infuriated, but their feelings were of no importance to me. Marcus pushed himself back in his chair, as if he was unsure of whether to intervene or not. Eventually he stood up and walked over to Antonio, attempting to get him to walk out of the room to talk, but Antonio brushed him off and turned to me.

"Liliana, you need to get dressed." Antonio said, slamming his hand upon the table, several times as he spoke. "You are going to delay us, and we all need to get to the airport as soon as possible."

He stood completely still when he was finished, gritting his teeth and clenching his fist together. I slowly looked up at him.

"I'm not going to the airport." I replied as I bit into an arepa with queso and wiped sour cream from the side of my mouth with a napkin, turning away from him, focusing only on the plate in front of me.

I didn't care if he was upset and I knew I was the only one at the table that felt that way at the moment. Chickens, I thought to myself. I was done being a chicken. Antonio watched me intently as I chewed my food and I paid no attention to him. I stared straight forward and focused on a tree in the distance that I could see from Elena's bay window. I managed to take another bite of food before he exploded.

"Liliana, you are acting ridiculous." He said loudly as he leaned over so that his face was close to mine. "You need to go upstairs and get ready."

I looked up at him, chewing the remainder of the food that I had in my mouth as I began to feel the anger growing stronger inside me. I clenched the side of the table with my left hand and shifted in my chair.

"You are spitting on my food." I replied angrily, as I tried desperately to get myself to relax.

Elena gasped as she tried to remain calm. Of course she would gasp, I thought to myself. My grip on the table tightened and when he didn't move, his face was still extremely close to mine and when I looked into his eyes, I saw my own eyes reflecting the anger that he was putting on display for the family. As I looked deep into his eyes, I could see the veins in his eyes turning red with furry, but that only added fuel to the fire that was burning within me.

"Lily, I'm not playing around with you right now." Antonio said loudly. "Is that what you are planning to wear when we board the airplane to Chicago?"

"I told you that I'm not going." I replied, pushing the words out from between my teeth.

The table was silent as everyone else waited for his reply. For several moments he said nothing. Neither of us did. Our eyes were locked on one another's gaze as we waited for the others next move. I told myself that I wasn't waiting, that was for sure. I may have had my eyes focused on his, but during this time I was already planning what I was going to say to my father when I met him, because I knew that was exactly what I was going to do next! If Antonio thought anything different, he was out of his mind. Antonio read my thoughts and his intense gaze appeared to loosen slightly.

"Liliana, your father knows we were leaving for Chicago." Antonio said, "It doesn't make any sense for you to stay here. Besides I don't want you to be alone with him, he's an extremely dangerous person and none of us know what he's capable of."

I shook my head and continued to stare at him.

"I don't know what you're capable of." I said through gritted teeth.

"Lily, he's back in Venezuela now." Antonio said. "I do know that he's busy. There's no point of you wanting to stay in Colombia he's not going to have time to meet with you."

I shook my head as I stared at him, but loosened my expression slightly. My father wouldn't have made the effort to get in contact with Antonio if he didn't want to meet me. I knew that, that was common sense.

"I need to hear that from him Antonio." I responded. "In the event that he does not have time to meet with me, I won't be upset, but you need to know that I also will not be going to Chicago with you and your family."

"Lily, why are you talking like this?" Antonio asked, throwing his hands up. "They're your family too."

I shook my head and shrugged as I stared blankly at him.

"Family indicates that there is a bond between us." I replied. "Family protects each other, looks out for each other and doesn't keep secrets from one another."

"We were protecting you." Elena said softly from across the table.

Antonio spun around and stared at her, indicating that this was not the time for her to get involved.

"I'm not leaving you in Colombia alone." Antonio said loudly, turning back to me. "You don't know how dangerous he is. Do you know that it's said that he's killed several of his own family members?"

I shrugged again. The fact was that I had some kind of an idea how dangerous this man was. I could see it on every one of Antonio's family member's faces whenever my father's nick name was mentioned. I didn't care about what his reputation was. He was my father, bound to me by blood, having the answers to questions that I was dying to ask him and I had to meet him.

"Can you just call him when we get to Chicago?" Antonio asked.

"No, I can't." I replied. "I'm not going anywhere, unless it is back home or to my father's house."

I let out a long sigh, as I looked around the table. I couldn't believe that I was having this discussion with him in front of so many of his family members, but that was his decision.

"Antonio, I don't want to be with you right now." I said sternly.

I gazed up at him, grabbing his attention with my eyes and pulling his gaze into my own.

"I can't be with you right now." I said lightly. "I have to meet my father."

The entire family sat aghast as the words left my mouth. The thought of me wanting to meet with El Jefe, suddenly seemed more alarming to them than for me to simply contact him. Had they thought that I wouldn't want to meet my father? Had they thought that a simple apology from Antonio would put everything that I had just learned in the past? Had they even bothered to apologize to me? What made them think that they weren't wrong for their part in keeping this major secret from me? I rolled my eyes as I looked around the table. Who did they think they were? Who did any of them think they were?

"Absolutely not." Antonio screamed back at me. "There is no way that you are going to meet with that man. He is pure evil and I won't have my wife be a part of it."

"That man is my father." I replied, my voice rising with each word that left my mouth. "Better yet, he is the only person in my family who has not lied to me or withheld any information from me. Maybe I shouldn't be your wife if there is a problem with your wife meeting with him."

"He hasn't had the chance to lie to you yet." Antonio screamed. "Do you think that makes him any different than the rest of us? No one intentionally tried to hurt you, everyone was trying to keep you from being hurt. Don't you understand that?"

I stood up quickly and pushed my plate to the side and slammed my own fist onto the table, leaning forward and coming face to face with Antonio.

"Listen Antonio, if you don't want to give me my father's contact information that is fine." I said, gritting my teeth as I spoke. "But I will tell you this, I am going to get in contact with him if I have to walk the streets of Colombia and ask every person that I pass, until I find someone that can tell me how to find him! I am going to meet my father. That is a fact and that is not something that you nor anyone at this table is going to take away from me!"

I looked around the table as I spoke and Antonio backed away from me.

"I'm sure that there are quite a few people on the streets in town that know how I can find him." I said harshly.

I raised my eyebrows and tilted my head to the right, never losing eye contact with him.

"And when I find him, I might even go to visit him in Venezuela." I said, "I'm not sure yet."

"Don't be stupid." Antonio said slowly from across the table.

I didn't pay attention to him and stood up straight as I proceeded, holding up my hand and counting my fingers as I continued.

"Let me see." I said. "I can start at the market, and then at the restaurant, he must eat when he's here, huh?"

I smiled a very odd smile that scared me and must have scared him, because I could feel him stare straight at me as he analyzed my reaction.

"There is also that block just south of the market that is filled with drug users and prostitutes, I can go there." I said in a lighter tone. "Someone has to know him there."

"Liliana you are talking like you are crazy now." Elena chimed in.

"I'm talking like I'm crazy?" I asked, my body swinging around to her as I spoke. "Get this into your head everyone, I am crazy."

I threw my hands up in the air to show my aggravation.

"I'm crazy to be standing in a room with all of you!" I shouted at her, but not specifically intending for her to be my target. "I'm crazy to be married into a family of murderers that don't care enough about people's lives, even when they are a part of this family."

I looked Antonio straight in his eye.

"How could you?" I asked sadly. "How could you kill anyone and still be able to live with yourself?"

I shook my head.

"You almost killed me that night and now I'm expected to be accepting of all of this?" I asked, staring at everyone at the table individually as I spoke. "I'm expected to accept this as a lifestyle that is normal?"

"Liliana, please calm down." Antonio said, suddenly appearing worried.

He reached out as if to attempt to take my hand in his. I looked down at it as it lingered in air, inches away from my own and stared at it for what felt like a solid minute. I finally shook my head.

"This is not what I want my life to stand for Antonio." I said lightly. "This is not me and I'm not willing to mold myself into thinking that it is okay."

My eyes burned with trapped tears, not willing to fall from the corners of my eyes. I turned and walked out of the room, I could feel Antonio following close behind me. He grabbed my arm the second he had the chance and I shook it away from him, turning to stare at him forcefully. Antonio stared straight at me.

"Well maybe we'll do that." Antonio finally replied. "Maybe we'll let you meet your father and then you can think over what you are implying when you are talking about our family. Let's see what you really think about your father and the rest of us then."

Blanca shook her head and looked down at the table and Elena seemed to sink in her seat. I knew that they didn't agree with Antonio's statement.

"I need my father's number." I said slowly. "I need to figure out who I am before I can go on with the rest of my life. Everything that I thought I knew has been taken away from me!"

I felt my shoulders sink.

"Everything that life has ever given me is always taken away from me." I said, fighting the urge to break into tears. I turned away briefly, as I tried to regain my strength.

"Lily, calm down mami." Antonio said softly. "Everything is going to be okay, it's going to work itself out, you'll see."

I swung around and stared him straight in the eye, a look so powerful, I was positive that he felt as if I had just stabbed him.

"Is my mother here? Can anything bring her back?" I asked. "No, then everything is not going to be ok? How can you even suggest that?"

"Liliana, you have the baby to think about." Antonio said, obviously giving up on trying to convince me to forgive him.

I sighed, leaning back and put my hand to my forehead. I hadn't forgotten that I was pregnant, but I knew I needed to keep my cool for the baby's sake. I shook my head.

"Antonio." I replied, fighting angry tears. "I need to talk face to face with my father. I don't care if you have to rent a helicopter and bring him here yourself, but you need to make it happen. Are we on the same page here?"

I grabbed his hands and looked him straight in the eyes.

"I need this Antonio." I said. "I need this more, than anything that I could ever ask of you or that you can ever give me."

Antonio stood before me without saying a word.

"I deserve that much." I said lightly. "I need to sit down with my father. I have so much to ask him."

Antonio looked at me for a moment, before removing his hands from my grasp and turning away. He sighed and put his hand to his forehead. It had worked. I could see it. I felt anxiousness begin to grow as my stomach seemed to flip-flop several times. He shook his head and took three steps away from me. His footsteps echoed loudly in the hallway. He slowly reached in his pocket, took out his cell phone and stared at it for what felt like minutes. I could feel the tension in the room growing and glanced around the table to study everyone's reactions. It was obvious that they knew what was coming too and none of them looked like they were happy about it.

Moments later, Antonio quickly dialed a number and walked out of the room, talking quickly in Spanish. I clasped my hands together and smiled a genuine smile. He was doing it. He was setting up the meeting with my father. I nervously walked out of the room, rubbing my belly as I walked and retreated to the living room, also filled with younger family members. I didn't look directly at any of them, but sat down as if nothing had happened.

Chapter Four

Ever so slowly the younger family members excused their selves and went outside. Before long, only those family members that were closest to Antonio and I began coming into the room without saying a word. Elena and Miguel, both appeared to be mad, but I couldn't tell if they were angry with me or with one another. Their eyes never met mine as they entered and they retreated to the furthest corner of the living room, their daughters following in seconds later ever so quietly. Roberta and Marcus did the same. Everyone was waiting to see what Antonio had to say when he came back and I only prayed that their reaction to his decision wouldn't cause further argument.

Within minutes Antonio walked into to the living room followed by his father. I stood up and walked over to the two of them in anticipation. Antonio turned to me and told me that the meeting with my father had been arranged. I suddenly felt a burst of happiness and hugged him quickly. He stared down at me as I did and I couldn't tell from his expression what he was thinking so I pulled away and sat down on Elena's oversized sofa and put my hand to my chest. I couldn't help but smile as I stared around the room at the expressions of the other family members. I felt like my heart was going a mile a minute. For a long while no one smiled back or dared to utter a word. The room was completely quiet, not even Elena's daughters who sat beside her and Miguel said a word.

I looked down and blew out my breath, trying to keep myself calm. I didn't know what to do or what to think. Antonio stood watching me as if he couldn't believe he had just arranged the meeting with my father. I was proud of myself for being strong with Antonio, yet at the same time, I was suddenly overcome with fright in meeting my father. I remembered my first interaction with the man that I previously knew as my father and didn't want to go through anything like that again. I could feel my heart begin to beat violently within my chest. I sighed and lead back on the sofa, feeling as if I would pass out from emotion. Antonio noticed my reaction and immediately came to my side.

"Lily, I can postpone the trip for a day or so." Antonio said. "The rest of the family will go to Chicago and I will stay here with you."

He wrapped his arm around my shoulders, I could feel his muscles flex as I looked up at him. His eyes appeared convincing, but I shook my head. As I looked at him, I couldn't help seeing the eyes of a killer that I had looked into at that stoplight so long ago.

"You and everyone else need to go to Chicago Antonio." I said grabbing his free hand as I spoke and squeezing it, with all my strength. "I need to do this on my own."

I paused and studied his reaction.

"I need some time away from you to let everything sink in." I continued.

Antonio nodded as I spoke, shaking his head as if he couldn't believe what was happening.

"This has been too much for me to even attempt to understand right now." I said, turning to the rest of the family and showing that my words were intended for every one of them.

Elena and my gaze met and she immediately looked away, her hands crossed upon her chest. Of all people, I expected her to be more understanding of the situation. Marcus nodded his head when our gaze met. Roberta, who leaned against the wall next to him, shook her head and walked out of the room. I wasn't expecting everyone to understand my decision, because not even I understood it. However, I did not expect the reaction that I got from Elena and Roberta. Antonio rubbed my left shoulder, as he sat down next to me. I knew he was fighting to get out whatever it was that he had to say.

"I've arranged for him to come here today." Antonio said, forcing a brief smile. "He will be at our house later this evening."

Elena shook her head and walked out of the room, leaving Miguel and the girls in the living room looking dumbfounded. Roberta ran after her from across the hall, the noise from her high heels ringing throughout the hallway. I smiled through tears as I looked up at Antonio and nodded my head. He rubbed my shoulder and we sat quietly to the dismay of everyone else in the room. Antonio's father did not appear happy, but remained at his side.

I knew that Antonio must have felt proud of himself for getting my father to come. He sat beside me, as if he were the only one able to protect me from all the bad in the world. I wondered if arranging the meeting had been all that difficult.

"He's not coming here." Miguel said from across the room. "Ever. Make sure your wife is aware of that."

No Turning Back

Miguel stood up and left the room, his daughters following quickly behind him. The youngest daughter's curly hair bouncing up and down in her ponytail as she walked. Even she appeared mad as she walked out of the room and toward their cousins who stood in the hallway trying to console their mother. Antonio's cousins shook their head in agreement.

"He is going to meet with you back at the house." Antonio said, pausing as he spoke. "You can stay there. We'll go without you."

An uproar went through the room.

"I can't believe your even thinking of letting that man come to your house primo." One of the cousins said, stepping forward from the hallway and shaking his head.

His cousin's eyes appeared so fierce it seemed that he wanted to fight Antonio over his decision. Antonio shook his head, seeming to calm down as time passed, despite the glances that his cousins threw him from across the room.

"Enrique, please." Antonio said. "This is my decision."

His cousin through up his right hand.

"This is your wife's decision." His cousin said. "Not yours. Don't get confused"

Antonio gritted his teeth and sat back.

"It's her father." Antonio said. "She wants to meet him and my house is the safest place for the meeting to take place. I made that decision, don't you let yourself be confused."

"Cabron." His cousin muttered.

I felt Antonio's arm move slightly from behind my head and I immediately sat back and put my hand on his leg to stop him from getting up.

"Antonio," I said. "The house sounds like a good idea. I'd like to get back there as soon as possible."

Blanca's mom walked in from the hallway and walked across the room, staring out the window briefly and holding her hands together as she thought over whether or not she wanted to confront me.

"This trip was supposed to be for the entire family." Blanca said from across the room. "It wasn't just for us."

"Not this time Blanca." I responded. "I can't let it go that easily."

Antonio shook his head, not removing his eyes from me.

"You are not to be left alone with him Liliana." Antonio said. "That is my only rule. I know that you don't believe it, but he is an evil man and he has a lot of enemies here as well as in Venezuela."

I looked around the room, suddenly feeling anger coming over to me and blood rushing to the tips of my ears. I felt hurt and I didn't know why.

"I want to be the judge of whether my father is evil or not." I said through my teeth as I stared back at him.

The room was silent, but I could see several family members shake their head in disgust. One of the maids entered and shook her head helplessly as she stared at Antonio. Antonio nodded and stood up, walking away from me. He quickly ordered her to pull out my suitcase from the stack, letting her know that I was headed back to the house. He then called out to Gilbert and asked him to start bringing the rest of the suitcases that were in the hallway to the car. The room soon divided up as everyone began to tend to their own belongings, suddenly forgetting the commotion in the room and all of the trouble that my decision had caused.

Antonio looked back at me angrily as I sat on the couch waiting for him to give me further instructions of how to attend my visit with my father, but instead he said nothing and his silence hurt me. I stood up and walked into the next room, where I knew the nanny was preparing the kids for the trip. I stooped down to their height as they played with their toys and hugged and kissed the two of them several times, laughing with them as they showed me their hands and tried to count their fingers in Spanish. Blanca and Antonio walked into the room behind me and Blanca began to gather up their things and hand them off to the maid, who was standing with an open diaper bag allowing Blanca to drop different things into it. Blanca went over a list with the nanny and then turned to me.

"I guess I will be their mother for a couple of months while we're in Chicago." Blanca said. "Someone has to be responsible for them."

"You will be their Grandmother." Was my quiet reply as I gritted my teeth, feeling my temperature rise. "Just as you always are."

Blanca and the nanny each took one of the children from me and began to carry them out. Tears welled in my eyes as I watched Antonio helplessly.

"This is what you wanted." Antonio said harshly, walking over to me and staring me intently in my eye as if it would change my mind.

I knew he was trying to break me down, they all were. I turned away from him, already beginning to second guess my decision to stay behind. *Was I doing the right thing?* I wondered. I heard high heels clopping down the hallway and looked up to see Elena as she entered the room. She hesitated as she watched us and Antonio turned away from me. The tension in the room was high and she said nothing as she watched Antonio and me.

"You know you are tearing your family apart." Elena said harshly.

I shook my head. I knew that I wasn't and regardless of what she had just said, Elena came to my side and tried to hug me. I shrugged her off and felt bad doing it. She was taken back but said nothing as she stepped away from me. I didn't have the courage to look her in the face as she waited for our eyes to meet. I felt horrible in a way, but I felt worse knowing the secret that the entire family had kept from me. I felt as though she had betrayed me.

"I asked you if you knew what you were getting into when you married into this family." Elena said quickly and stepped away from me.

Her lip quivered, as if she wanted to say more but she said nothing. Antonio went to Elena's side and put his arm around her shoulders, leading her out of the room, her curly hair smashed down against her neck under his grip. I silently followed them as they walked down the hallway and to the front door. As they prepared to leave, Antonio instructed his parent's driver to take me back to the house as soon as I was ready and had his parents get into our car with the twins and the nanny. Blanca was not happy and she made it clear to everyone around her, as she went over everything with the nanny once more before getting into the car.

As I stood at the doorway, Blanca eyed me without saying a word. Antonio Salvador stood at the side of the car, waiting for a reaction from either me or Antonio. Antonio Salvador's eyes looked just as apologetic as Antonio's did. When neither of us said anything Antonio Salvador climbed into the car.

My heart felt like it was breaking as I watched everyone prepare to leave. The twins' waved good bye, before being put into their car seats and it made my heart crumble. In spite of the pain that I immediately began to feel I knew that I had to do this. Antonio didn't say anything to me as he prepared to join the rest of his family.

"You don't have to do this by yourself." He muttered as he stared at me.

I nodded my head and stared back at him.

"Yes I do." I said briskly.

In spite of what I was feeling, I didn't dare show him or any of the rest of the family a clue as to how excruciating the pain that I felt within my soul. Antonio grabbed my chin in his fingers and kissed me on the forehead and pulled away without saying another word. My heart felt like it melted in his grasp. I walked him to the car, watching hesitantly as he got in. He turned and smiled at me one last time, his smile making me want to run to him and hold him. Instead I backed away from the car, my hands folded across my chest, immediately feeling lost and alone. One of the maids coming to my side, watching with me as the car pulled out. I was unsure of what my next move would be. I didn't know what meeting my father would lead to. I could only hope that we would have a good relationship and that he wasn't as evil a person as everyone made him out to be.

Chapter Five

The maids at our house seemed surprised when I pulled up in the car at the gate without Antonio and even more surprised that I strolled into the house wearing my pajamas and robe. I was sure that Antonio had called them to let them know that I was on my way home. I acted as though I didn't notice them glance at each other as I walked past them. They could at least be more discreet about it, I thought to myself. Rather than rush to get ready, I lay down on the sofa and did absolutely nothing until noon. I carefully thought about the questions that I had for my father and asked them aloud, to gain confidence.

When I heard the grandfather clock strike the twelve o'clock mark I sat up very slowly, noticing one of the maids watching me from a separate room. She must have thought that I was crazy. She quickly turned and ran off to the other room, soon afterward another maid came out with lunch. I thanked her and stared down at my food. It felt weird being in the house without Antonio, or the kids. I quickly ate my food, finishing and slowly making my way upstairs. I felt misplaced and alone. *This was my choice*, I reminded myself. I would have to learn to make the best of it.

I climbed into the shower and within minutes I was thinking about how everything had played out within the last two days. I thought about how I had stood up to Antonio and the rest of his family, ultimately winning my own personal battle. By the time I was done with my shower, I felt like I had a new perspective on life. I was tired of being stepped on, unappreciated and ordered around. I knew I needed to start doing things for myself and this was just the beginning of my journey uphill. I shook my head, staring at my blank expression in the mirror. *I need to be serious about this*, I thought to myself. I wrapped a towel around my body, suddenly feeling empowered and alive.

"I can do this." I said, walking into my closet to get dressed.

Antonio's voice and his orders began to replay in my mind. I remembered how he told me that I was under no circumstance to be alone with my father. I shook my head as I put my clothes on thinking ever so hard on what Antonio said. At that moment I decided that if my father asked me to go with him to Venezuela, I would. I might even ask him to go back with him myself. I needed to get away from this place and from life as I knew it. Antonio didn't have to know if I left. After all, Antonio was on a plane to Chicago, he didn't have a choice in the matter. I walked out of my room and without meaning stomped down the stairway. The maids gathered around the foot of the stairs waiting for me to say something. I shook my head, staring back up at the top of the stairs, as if I was looking for an answer to their questioning expressions.

"My father is coming." I said lightly, looking at them and hoping they understood me.

I didn't want there to be any surprises. No one uttered a word and their expressions remained unchanged. I shook my head and walked past them and into the living room. Just once, I wished that someone around here besides a member of Antonio's family would talk to me. I needed to talk to someone that didn't have a predetermined side. I sat down on the sofa feeling full of frustration and stared at the painting of Antonio and me at our wedding that seemed to haunt our room from its place above the fireplace. I wondered if we would ever be a normal family, sighing as I sat lost deep in thought.

At three o'clock in the afternoon I received a call from my father's secretary, Alejandra. Her voice was soft, but her message got straight to the point as she told me that my father's car would be pulling up in twenty minutes. I jumped up as I spoke to her, suddenly feeling more nervous than I ever imagined possible. I let out a long sigh, the moment I hung up the phone with her and plopped back down on the sofa. In minutes, I would be meeting the man that everyone in Antonio's family seemed to despise.

I could hear the sound of the clock ticking as I waited for the famous "El Jefe" to arrive. The sounds of each second that passed seemed to echo loudly through the room. I felt nervous as I sat waiting for him, folding my hands on top of my long maroon skirt. I rubbed my hand against my belly in circles, as if that simple action would help calm me down. My stomach wasn't that big, if someone didn't already know I was pregnant, they wouldn't be able to tell. I wondered if my father knew, as I began to sweat profusely, immediately deciding not to wear my hair down and pulling it into a tight bun. I glanced at my hand as if I wore a watch and then quickly looked up at the large clock across the wall in the hallway. Time wasn't going quick enough, I thought to myself.

I changed positions several times; my right eye began to twitch from nervousness. Finally, I stood up and walked into the kitchen, pouring myself a large glass of juice, while the maids watched me in horror. I smiled lightly as I glanced over at them. They clung together watching me, without saying a word with wide eyes as if they were scared about something. I wondered if Antonio had called them to explain what was going on. They were probably horrified of what was going to happen when my father arrived.

"My father is coming in a few minutes." I said, in an attempt to make some kind of conversation with them.

They stared straight through me. Nothing changed. Not a single one of them uttered a word. I shook my head and walked out of the room. I didn't understand them and they didn't understand me. I wished Catalina was there to talk things out with. I was in desperate need to talk over what I was going to say to my father when he arrived. I walked into the living room and sat back down on the sofa, attempting to drink my glass of juice. My hand began shaking vigorously. I set the glass down on the table quickly and stared at it for several seconds. One of the maids came into the room as if she wanted to say something. When our eyes met she shook her head and quickly walked out of the room. *Was I making a mistake in wanting to meet this man?* I thought to myself again. I glanced across the room at the phone and questioned myself about calling back to cancel the meeting. I stood up momentarily as I watched the phone, before quickly sitting back down.

Finally I heard a car pull up to the gate. I raced to the window to peek out and moments later the buzzer rang to alert us that we had a guest. The maid entered the room and stood without saying anything for several moments. She cleared her throat to break the silence and I nodded to her so that she would call and request that the guards let the car in. She picked up the phone and called the guard, shaking her head as she did so, speaking very quickly and appearing as if she might run out of the room at any moment. I picked up my glass to take another drink, just as I heard the sound of the gate opening to let my father in. I debated on going to the door to greet him.

Seconds later I dashed to the door. I couldn't help myself. I already felt like I had been waiting too long. Loose strands of hair fell against my face as I stared at the car in exasperation. I blew my breath upwards in attempt to get them back in place, my hands going limp from nervousness. I was frustrated but tried to regain my composure as I walked out on our marble porch, overlooking the concrete pavement below. I began to walk down the stairs, telling myself to walk slowly, but walking faster with every step. A light breeze blew against me as I stood waiting at the bottom of the steps.

I turned and looked back at the house, seeing two of the maids lingering in the doorway. My body cringed as our eyes met and turned to walk further toward my father's car. By the time that the car door opened, I was already standing at the end of the sidewalk, at the side of my father's car. I felt out of control and stepped back a few steps to avoid appearing apprehensive. The Chauffer slowly got out of the car and chuckled at my anxiousness. My heart felt like it was going a mile a minute as I stood waiting for him to walk around the car and open the door for my father. The second my father stepped out of the car I nervously took the remaining two steps toward him.

He adjusted his tie the moment he was out of the car, giving me time to examine him. He was tall and dressed in a black suit with pinstripes that made him look even taller. Other than the fact that he was at least a foot taller than the man I originally knew as my father, the two looked identical. No wonder my mother had chosen the two of the men to be significant factors in her life. My father stood at the side of the car, watching me from behind a pair of black sunglasses and a broad smile spread across his face. He slowly reached up and took off his sunglasses, tucking them into his left pocket and stepped forward. I squinted my eyes as I stared at him. Something about him looked familiar to me. *Had I ever seen him before?* I quickly shook my head, pushing the idea out of my head and hesitantly stepped forward, forcing a light smile.

"Liliana," he said happily as I came closer to him, spreading his arms out to greet me.

I paused, not knowing what to do and he stepped forward and hugged me tightly in his arms, rubbing my back as he did so. I exhaled, feeling my body tighten up. I felt incredibly nervous and hadn't been expecting this warm embrace from a man that was hated by many. My father's grasp was gentle and loving, exactly what I imagined a father's embrace should feel like. It felt different than when Antonio hugged me. My body went weak and I didn't know what to say or do, finally managing to pull it together and hug him back. When we stepped away from each other we were both quiet and I wondered if he was as confused as I was. I could feel my palms begin to sweat, and I nervously fiddled with the rings on my left hand as I stood before him.

My father stepped back and smiled at me again. His teeth seemed to sparkle as his lips spread widely across his face. His face showed signs of his age, his forehead boasting wrinkles straight across it, rather than at the sides of his eyes, like my father in law. His skin was leathery and thick; the right side of his cheek had a deep scar on it. I felt the smile leave my face and my father pulled out his handkerchief and wiped a tear from his right eye. I stood watching him in disbelief, my lips slightly parted. I had it in my head that crying was a form of weakness and I didn't expect this fearless looking man to be weak. The wind blew lightly against us as we stood there watching each other in awe and waiting for the other to speak.

"You know, you are my only child." He said with a heavy accent.

I smiled lightly and glanced away. I didn't really know how to respond to that. My mind filled with questions of my own. I stood there trying to figure out the questions that were most important to me.

"What should I call you?" I asked nervously looking down as I spoke.

Really? I thought to myself. *Was that the best question you could come up with?* My father paused and then smiled at me harder than he had previously.

"Papi." He replied happily. "Or whatever you want to call me, as long as it's nothing too bad. I'm not really as bad as everyone thinks."

He winked, smiling harder than ever and pulled out a cigar. I stared at him without saying a word and he stepped back to smoke it away from me. My heart felt like it was melting. I wiped a tear that fell from my left eye, upset with myself because I was determined not to act like a baby and sure that my mascara was running down the side of my face.

"Are you sure about that?" I asked, showing my teeth as an uncontrollably wide grin spread across my face. "I mean, is it okay with you?"

"Oh, I'm positive." My father replied, dropping his cigar and stomping on it with his left foot. "It would make me the proudest man in the world."

He studied the cigarette butt he had smashed in the ground momentarily and then looked back up at me.

"Worst habit ever." He said more to himself than to me.

I starred at the cigarette butt before looking up at him.

"You don't smoke, do you?" My father asked.

I shook my head and studied his expression. I was too nervous to speak, my breath felt like it was trapped within my lungs and I didn't know what was wrong with me. I felt my hands begin to sweat uncontrollably and wiped them against the sides of my skirt. I tried to ask him a question, but none of the twenty questions that I had in my mind wanted to come out. My father stared at me for a moment without saying anything. He seemed to understand me by just looking at me and stepped back, glancing briefly back at the car, waving to the driver to go and park it.

"Let's go sit down and talk." My father said.

Chapter Six

I felt like a little girl again as I stared at my father. I smiled lightly and nodded as he took my hand and led me to the side of the house. We continued walking until we got to a stone bench that sat near a mound of Victoria cruziana flowers. I glanced back at my house and saw two of the maids watching us from the living room window. I quickly turned to my father and examined his expression, wondering if he had any idea how nervous I was. I couldn't help staring at him, as I tried my best to remember every detail about him. While I did this, I couldn't help noticing that my father wasn't a bad looking man. He didn't look as old, as I knew that he was.

"Your house is beautiful." My father said suddenly, breaking the silence.

I shifted slightly and smiled at him without saying anything.

"You probably have a million questions for me." He said after a moment. "Don't let them all out at once."

I smiled and nodded as my mind suddenly went blank. I didn't know what to say. I sat staring at him with a confused expression on my face for at least a minute before he again broke the silence and began to speak.

"I never knew about you, at the same time I always wondered." He said suddenly, as if he had just read my mind. "Do you know what I mean Liliana?"

I nodded my head and smiled lightly, beginning to feel some of the nervousness leave my system as I listened to his deep, yet soothing voice. My shoulders even seemed to loosen up as I sat listening to him.

"When did you figure it out?" I asked.

My father only smiled as he stared at me, squinting slightly from the sun.

"I spent a great deal of time thinking about your mother after she left me." He said and sighed heavily, studying my expression and shaking his head before continuing.

Did I tell him that he wasn't answering my question? I wondered. He looked away and then back at me as if he was debating making up his mind on whether to continue.

"I heard that you were sent to live with my cousin after your mother was killed. It got me thinking about her. Remembering things about her." My father paused. "Remembering things about us."

I smiled knowingly as I stared at him.

"I'm so sorry Liliana." My father said. "Let's be honest, I know that my cousin is a piece of shit. The first time I saw you, something in my heart told me that you were mine."

I blinked my eyes as I rethought what he had just said.

"Wait a minute." I said, holding up my right hand as if to stop him. "You saw me? When?"

I stared at him, suddenly feeling my heart turn to stone.

"When you walked into the restaurant with Antonio." My father explained, going off into thought momentarily. "It was such a long time ago now. You were soaking wet. It was before I knew anything about you, but it was what got me thinking that there was a possibility that you could be mine."

He smiled at the memory and squinted his eyes, trying to avoid looking at the sun as he spoke. My chest stiffened as I prepared myself to hear more.

"I was at a back table in the restaurant. I was with one of your uncles and my mutual cousins, when you and Antonio walked in." My father said. "Everyone knew who Antonio was but no one knew who you were."

My father smiled briefly.

"My cousin did though. He knew you from the neighborhood." My father laughed as he spoke. "You seemed terrified when you saw our cousin. You looked directly at him and didn't even notice me. You looked like you had just seen a ghost."

My father shook his head.

"My cousin had you that spooked. The fact is that it was me that felt like I had just seen the ghost." My father said. "You look so much like your mother and at the same time, a lot like my mother."

My father shook his head in disbelief.

"I felt my heart stop." My father said. "I asked Tito, our cousin all about you."

He shook his head again.

"Tito told me who you were, but even Tito didn't believe that you were our cousin's child." My father said. "Tito knew your mom. In fact he knew you when you were just a baby, before you went to America with your mom."

My father sighed.

"I can't believe that I didn't realize sooner." He said in a sad tone. "That night at dinner Tito made a comment about how he thought that you might be mine and I shook it off because I didn't think that it could be true."

I sighed heavily as those final words were spoken. If he had put two and two together back then, if he had realized that I was his daughter, I wondered if Antonio and I would be together now. I let out a deep breath without being able to pull together what I wanted to say. I felt disoriented at the thought. I could have been taken to live with him and at the same time have been taken out of harm's way. I wouldn't have needed Antonio's help and all of the secrets that were kept from me would remain just that.

"When you and Antonio were married, I came across your picture in the newspaper and then again when you gave birth to my grandsons." My father suddenly said. "Everything made sense and it made me so curious Liliana. I had to find out and I did."

I felt my shoulders droop down against my body unintentionally. So much was going through my mind. My heart pounded heavily as I listened to the words of his story. My mind was broken as I tried to analyze the statements he made. I wanted to shout at him. I wanted to ask him why he didn't follow up with his cousin any sooner. Things could have been so different I thought. Was it that he didn't want someone additional to worry about I wondered? I knew that I didn't exactly fit in with his picturesque lifestyle? I noticed my father studying my expression as I sat beside him. He paused briefly, as if to give me a chance to argue with him. When I didn't, he leaned in and continued.

"Liliana, I can't tell you that I sat at home wondering if you were mine, because I didn't and sweetheart, I am so sorry that I didn't." He said. "That's just me. I'm selfish. The more that you get to know me, the more that you'll realize that. I didn't have the time and I feel bad for saying it, but I didn't care."

He raised his eyebrows at me, as if to get his point across. I felt my eyes water up and I bit down on my lip hard. There was no way in the world that I was going to let this man see one of my tears. I fought my own reflexes severely and within seconds my eyes were dry.

"I had my business." He said softly, twiddling his thumbs nervously as he spoke. "I had women coming in and out when I needed them to. For me to have a child a girl at that, it just wasn't going to happen."

He shook his head.

"I'm a dog and that's just not me." He said, putting his hand to his chest. "It's embarrassing when I think about it now, extremely embarrassing, but I hope that you are willing to understand me and to at least try to understand my lifestyle."

He looked at the pond for a moment before continuing. I nervously changed positions, beginning to wonder where this conversation was leading.

No Turning Back

"I'm not a good guy Liliana." My father said. "I'm sure Antonio and his family have told you that and everything that they've told you is probably right. I can't try to be someone who I'm not and I'm not willing to change the person that I am."

"It sounds horrible, but what in the world would happen if it was known that I suddenly had a daughter? What if it was found out that I had grandkids?" He asked. "Do you think that you would be safe? I couldn't ask that of you. Now, maybe things are a little different, I've been laying low for a while and I really want to get to know you, in spite of the risk that we may be taking. It's different now, you're not a defenseless young woman anymore."

My father laughed nervously.

"You probably wouldn't have been sitting here today if you weren't willing to take the chance." My father said, answering his own question. "Back then you would have been in constant danger and that is one thing that I could never ask that of anyone, especially not my only daughter."

I held my breath to keep myself from exploding.

"Liliana, I don't have a fortress that protects me like you have here with your husband." My father said. "I live a very meager life and you need to know. I don't want you to think that by ever coming to visit me that you're going to live more luxuriously than you do now."

My father sat up straight and fidgeted with the sunglasses in his pocket.

"Sure I drive around in fancy cars but that's about it." My father said raising his eyebrows. "I do a very good job of blending in. A very good job."

He laughed out loud and I forced a smile. He pulled his sunglasses back out of his top left-hand pocket and put them on.

"When you come to visit me, you'll see what I have, or rather what I don't have and you'll hate it." He said. "You'll want to go right back home to your palace immediately."

I bit down on my lip and looked up at him, lightly shaking my head. How could he think that? I wondered. Did he not know that I had spent my first three years in Colombia sleeping on a straw bed?

"Anything that you could have offered me would have been better than what I had with your cousin." I finally muttered. "How could you leave me with him if you suspected that there was a chance that I might be your child?"

My father threw his hand to his head in aggravation.

"I was wrong, okay?" He said. "I admit it and I'm sorry for that."

He shook his head vigorously.

"I was wrong not to wonder." He said. "I was wrong not to chase after your mother when she left, but to be honest I hated her for leaving. Even worse I hated her for leaving with my cousin."

He grunted and sat back against the bench in dismay. How could I be allowing him to talk this way about my mother? Suddenly he reached forward and grabbed both of my hands in his.

"Liliana I have to be honest with you. You have to let me discuss how I feel. I know it bothers you but I did hate her."

My father said. "She ran off with my cousin. For her, I would have given the world, but she betrayed me. She acted as if she made a mistake in marrying me, but that's what she wanted."

"The two of you were married?" I asked, as I sat in shock.

That was something my mother had never told me. My father nodded. He paused briefly before continuing.

"If I would have known the heartache that she would later cause me, I would have left her with her parents long ago. I wouldn't have married her." My father explained, as he sat deep in thought.

"Well maybe I would have." He said suddenly. "The fact is Liliana, I was in love with her from the moment I saw her and she took that love and used it against me. When she left, she took my heart with her and all the love that I could ever feel for anyone! "

He slammed his fist to his chest as he said the last words.

I looked away for a moment and noticed the maids quickly jump out of view as they watched us from the window.

"She looked just like an angel." My father said. "I would have never, in a hundred years, imagined that she would hurt me the way that she did."

I sat deep in thought as I listened to him.

"I'm sorry." I muttered without knowing why.

My father shook his head as if to tell me that it was alright.

"She was an angel." He said. "She was just not my angel."

He shook his head as he watched and seemed to analyze my expression.

I sat staring blankly at him. I could see the hurt in his eyes as he spoke about her.

"Why her?" I asked suddenly. "Why my mom? What attracted you to her?"

He shook his head again as if he didn't know what to tell me.

"I mean she was so young." I blurted out. "Was her family okay with that? Was your family okay with that?"

"Why not? My family was fine with us." He replied. "They were more concerned with what her parents thought of the situation or what they might do to stop us."

He smiled suddenly and looked up at me his eyes glistening.

"She was here with her parents visiting and I met her at the beach." He started off, raising his lip for a moment.

"She looked a lot older than she was." He said. "A lot older. I thought she was at least eighteen at the minimum."

I shook my head and smiled. I could imagine my mother as a teenager. I hadn't seen any pictures of her, but I remembered her telling me that she had always looked older.

"I should have figured out that she was younger than I thought she was, when her parents left her at the hotel and took her brother and sister out to a local event." My father said thoughtfully. "I remember that her mother, your grandmother was totally against taking them, to the event but your grandfather wanted your aunt and uncle to have a good time while they were here. Your mom said she was fine with hanging around the pool all day and that was the end of it."

He smiled again, a wide grin spreading across his face.

"Your grandmother actually said that your mother had to stay at the hotel because she would get into too much trouble if she came along. In all actuality, they didn't know how much trouble your mother was going to get in to staying behind." My father said, chuckling as he spoke.

He looked away for a moment.

"I saw her at the pool and we got to talking." My father said. "I don't want to get into details, but one thing led to another and before I knew it, I was in her room."

"What?" I exclaimed, shaking my head.

I couldn't imagine my mother jumping into bed with someone so fast! I didn't know what to think.

"You're old enough for me to tell you this." He said raising his hands. "Let me know if you want me to stop."

He paused as he waited for my reply. I stared back at him as I felt my heart expand in my chest. It depended on what he had to tell me, I thought to myself. I shook my head, feeling confused. I was almost scared of what he was about to say as his lips parted.

"I didn't know it when I met her." My father continued. "It was her first time, she didn't want to tell me, and I didn't know until it was impossible for me not to be able to tell. I fell in love with her immediately and I questioned her."

He looked around, as if to see if anyone else was listening.

"She blurted out her age and spilled her guts about everything, including how scared she was that her parents would know." He said. "She was worried about what they would do if they found out and I looked at her differently. I saw her as a little girl and I decided that since I had already done the damage, I had to have her."

I raised my eyebrows as he spoke. I didn't know if I wanted him to continue.

"I convinced her to run away with me. I wanted to protect her and she was all for the idea at the time." He said. "When we got back home, I told everyone that she was my wife and that was it. A week later she was crying to go back home, which made my family question what had really happened and begin to worry about what her parents thought. Their questioning became really annoying, so I took both her and my younger cousin and the three of us moved into our own apartment."

I was astonished, as I sat listening to his side of the story, secretly wishing that my mother was here so that she could cut in and tell me that this was not how it happened. I leaned into my father as he spoke, not wanting to miss a single detail. As he went on, I became lost in his words. I was in my own world as I listened, visualizing my mother nod as if she was showing that she was sorry that I was finding out about her troubled ways via my father.

Chapter Seven

As I sat listening to my father, I felt my feelings starting to change toward him. I could visualize everything that he was discussing with me and I tried to record everything that he was telling me in my mind.

"Liliana, I wasn't the person that I am today." My father said. "I was some stupid eighteen year old, hanging out on the streets trying to make money to support us, coming home whenever I wanted to. Your mother left with my cousin a few months later."

He looked away momentarily, raising his lip again.

"It was my fault that she left me, but I still hated her for leaving." My father said. "Who would have thought that my own cousin would stab me in the back like that?"

I stared at him in shock. I didn't know what to think. I was glad that he was being so open and honest with me, but at the same time I didn't want to hear everything that he was telling me. I had always thought very highly of my mother and I didn't want him to change my opinion of her. I shuttered at the thoughts that began to go through my mind. I was visualizing everything. I squirmed uncomfortably on the bench as the two of us sat gazing across the grass. Before I could say anything my father leaned toward me and put his arm around me as if he was trying to comfort me.

"You know, I think that she tried to tell me about you." He said. "There's a phone call that I can't get out of my head."

I glanced over at him and forced a smile.

"One day I was with a woman that I had brought back over to my place." My father started off. "There was a phone call and your mother called, crying into the receiver. Your mother and my cousin had just arrived in America and were told that her entire family had died in a plane crash while they were returning from Colombia."

He snarled his lips as he spoke.

"She had inherited a small amount of money." My father continued. "She started off by telling me that."

He looked over at me, his expression turned to one of guilt as he went on.

"Why are you telling me this? I asked. I told her that I didn't care." He said. "In the background I could hear a baby babbling and she tried to stop me. She tried to tell me that she had something really important to tell me."

He paused briefly, looking away.

"At that point I didn't want to hear her." He said angrily. "The sound of her voice irritated the hell out of me. Especially knowing that she was in the United States with my cousin. It ate at my soul and I hung up the phone just like that."

He looked over at me, as if to ask for approval. When I did nothing, he sighed and looked straight ahead at the grass, and an odd expression appearing on his face.

"That's when I lost my soul. I didn't care anymore." My father said. "She called again and again, but I wouldn't take her calls. I had my lady friend answer the phone and yell at her, telling her to stop calling. I wanted her to feel the same pain that I felt. I wanted to hurt her as much as she hurt me."

He sighed heavily, as if he regretted what he was about to tell me.

"You know Liliana; she actually sent me a letter with a picture once. I nearly burned it." He said, reaching into his back pocket and retrieving his wallet. "I've always kept it. Not because I knew what it was, but out of spite."

He opened his wallet and revealed a picture of my mother and me as a baby. I gasped and immediately put my hand to my mouth, reaching over and taking the picture from him. He smiled at me as I looked at it with tears streaming from my eyes.

"You know I never read the letter." He said. "I tore it up immediately. The picture I kept in order to remind me never to fall in love again."

He laughed.

"When I felt myself getting to close to someone, I took out the picture and got over it." He said gruffly. "I never really looked at the baby in the picture as if it was mine. You were too young to see any similarities."

He reached over and wiped my eyes lightly with his handkerchief, and then taking the picture back and putting it carefully back into the wallet.

"Who would have known? Now I kick myself for not reading the letter." He said, letting out a light laugh as he did.

I smiled lightly, before biting my lips together. I was overcome with emotion and had never felt so confused in my life. I sat staring into the eyes of this man, hated by many, quite possibly a terrible person and yet he was still my father. I didn't know how I felt about that. I didn't know whether or not I wanted to let him into my life. I did know that I wanted to know more about him and any information that he could give me on my family. I let out a light sigh to release some of the tension that was building within my chest.

"I don't know what made me want to find out if those boys were my grandsons but when I found out that Antonio had ordered a test to find out if he was their father, I decided to get a hold of the results." He said. "It wasn't hard to do, either. When the test results came back with a good deal of probability that your boys were my grandkids, I made my cousin take the test."

My father grasped his chest.

"I was devastated Liliana. Rather than to be happy, all that I could feel was grief." He said. "I felt so much guilt and I didn't know why. I was a lady's man, heart cold as stone. At least I thought I was. I told myself that things could have been different, but the fact is, you wouldn't have been any better off. I was young and immature."

He sighed lightly.

"Your mother did a good job raising you. She was really a good woman." He said. "I'm sorry that my cousin had to mess it up for you. I'm sorry that I had to mess it up for you."

We both smiled at that sentiment. I knew as well as he did that there was no way to take back the past. We could only move forward. I had accepted hurt and anguish from Antonio as my husband, but I wasn't sure that I could accept it from my father.

"Liliana, mija, look at me." He said. "I want you to know how serious I am when I say this."

I was already looking at him, but I stared deep into his eyes.

"I'm ready to do whatever it takes to be your father." He said to me convincingly. "I'll do whatever it takes, if you'll let me."

During the time Antonio was gone, our phone conversations were brief. I was still hurt by learning the fact that he killed my mother and questioning myself as far as how I could go on with our relationship. I felt like the only thing that was keeping me in Colombia was that I loved my children and I didn't want our family to be torn apart permanently. Every hour being away from the twins felt like a life time.

Later that day, Antonio called me to ask how the meeting with my father went and I simply told him I appreciated him organizing our meeting for us. I was short with him and that of course didn't stop Antonio from asking more questions. I held my ground and didn't answer any of them. I asked him to put the boys on the phone and when I was done speaking with them I abruptly hung up the phone.

It was none of his business about anything my father and I had discussed. Still, I wished that Antonio and I were on good terms right now because I really felt like I needed someone to talk to. My heart hurt when I thought about the things my father told me about my mother and I was still debating on whether or not I wanted to believe that they were true. The whole situation still didn't feel believable to me. How could I have been led to believe for so long that someone else was my father? How could no one have cared enough to tell me and how were any of the events in my life decided? What was God's plan for me?

Antonio didn't let up, after an hour or so he called back and every hour on the hour after that. He wanted to know more information about the meeting with my father. He wanted to fix our relationship and thought that by talking to me I would magically fall back in to his arms. No! I was done being controlled by everyone else. Why didn't anyone get it? When he asked me if my father and I planned to meet again, I told him I wasn't sure. When he asked if my father had tried to contact me, I told him he hadn't, regardless of the fact that he had. Over the next week my father began calling me almost as frequently as Antonio did. This only made it more and more obvious to me that my father wanted to establish a relationship with me, which made me more and more upset that Antonio was trying to prevent it.

I kept details about my day simple with Antonio and pushed him away more and more. I didn't ask him questions about anything that was going on in Chicago, aside from how the kids were doing and our repetitive conversations were beginning to annoy me. I finally told Antonio that if he wanted me to get over the whole situation with my mother I needed my space. He backed off immediately, decreasing his calls to one a day or every other day.

At the same time, my father's calls increased, which was not to any of the maids liking. In fact they made it obvious that they didn't approve of my father's visits by being blatantly rude to me after he left our house or I hung up the phone with him. I didn't understand what their problem was; they didn't even look at me when I walked around in our house other than that. Why was it that everyone thought that my business was their business I wondered? When my father came over to visit, they made themselves scarce, watching us from a distance shaking their heads whenever I looked their way, talking amongst themselves quietly in the kitchen and snubbing me when I passed by them in the hallway.

To me their opinions and those of everyone else were unimportant. I made my own decision that I wanted to know my father. I only had one living parent and I intended to know everything that I could about him. When I was with my father I felt a sudden rush of power, that I had trouble explaining, even to myself. I suddenly was able to put pieces of my life together, that I was never able to before and I was able to figure out my background and who my family was. This was something that I had not been mature enough to do with my mother and something that I regretted.

I began to feel like there was nothing and not anyone in the world who could keep me away from my father. When I was around him, I was happy. I felt like a little girl again. There was so much to learn from each of his visits. When his car pulled up at the gate, I stood at the door waiting for him to circle the drive like a puppy, a new list of questions in mind to ask him. In fact, the closer I grew to my father, the further away from Antonio I felt.

When Antonio called on the phone, my chest froze and my body cringed. I couldn't stand the sound of his voice and it pained me to talk to him. What was I going to do when he came home? I was beyond distraught. Antonio was still my husband, but I had already accepted so much from Antonio and felt that there had to be a point where I would draw the line. I knew that praying had to be the answer but as much as I prayed or asked for guidance, I still felt like I was completely lost and it didn't help any to realize that in spite of everything, I still loved Antonio.

No Turning Back

If I decided to stay with Antonio, I felt like I was betraying my mother. If I decided to leave him I felt like I was betraying my family. I didn't want my children to grow up without both of us in their life. I felt like I owed it to them to protect them from having a childhood similar to my own. Antonio was a wonderful father, he had just been a horrible husband in the past, but over the last year and aside from this major family secret, he had really changed. I wanted this relationship to work out. I grew up having so many questions. Even to this day there were pieces of my life that could never be mended and I didn't want that for my children.

My feelings were the same for Elena and the rest of the family. I knew that no matter how close Elena and I were, Antonio was her brother and she would do whatever she could to protect him and to keep us together. I thought about that as I sat staring blankly at the wall and questioned myself as to whether or not I would have come forward with the information if the shoe had been on the other foot. I shook my head as I sat lost in thought. Who was I to trust? I lay back on my bed and closed my eyes, hoping and praying for an answer.

Chapter Eight

Within three weeks of meeting my father, he convinced me to come and stay with him the remainder of the time Antonio and the rest of our family were gone. This would mean travelling to Venezuela, a country that I had been warned about time and time again. Despite knowing this, I decided to go. This was somewhere that my mother had lived and somewhere that I might find more information out about her or about myself. I packed my bags without any of the maids noticing. I knew they were reporting my movements to Antonio, I could tell from the conversations that we had. I grabbed my bags and threw them out the window, knowing that moments later my father would arrive.

My heart pounded as I walked out of the room. Why was I so worried I wondered, I was an adult now. I nearly turned back around the moment I stepped out onto the stairs and saw the maids gathered in the entry way. *Pull yourself together,* I thought to myself, as I continued down the stairway. As I approached them they turned and stared at me. None of them smiled, their expressions made me think they knew I was up to something. I mentioned to Vanessa, one of the maids that I was going to dinner with my father and she nodded. Two of the other maids immediately turned their backs and walked toward the kitchen. I knew that Vanessa had the biggest mouth out of the three and that she was the one who was most likely to tell Antonio my whereabouts.

No Turning Back

When I heard the guards call to say that my father had arrived, I quickly went outside to grab my bag from the ground below my window. My father got out of the car and I nodded at him. He walked over and took my bags, looking back at the house as if he knew that I had thrown them from my window moments before. I smiled and quickly hugged him before getting in the car. I glanced over my shoulder as he handed my bags to the driver and loaded them into the back and breathed a sigh of relief. I didn't think anyone had seen my bags, the curtains were all closed and I didn't notice anyone peeking out from behind them. I smiled and turned back to my father, exhaling heavily to show my relief. I had managed to get in the car with my bags, without anyone noticing that I was leaving. I realized what I may be getting myself into, but at this point I was ready to turn over another page of my life. I left for Venezuela that night knowing that my trip would be a problem.

The difference with going to Venezuela was that, unlike Antonio and Elena who lived in a rural area, my father lived in the heart of the city. He lived near the hills overlooking the west end of the city. Luckily he didn't live too far west, just far enough to make the area a bad one, but not terrible. Just like Colombia there was minimal difference between the rich and the poor. My dad, unlike Antonio lived alongside the poor who mainly resides in the west end of the city and just being here, was apparent that even though I was raised in Chicago, city life was very different here.

My father was accustomed to seeing many of the things that made my mouth drop as we drove past. I couldn't imagine how much worse it was on the bad areas of the city that my father talked about avoiding, but I couldn't imagine it being worse than what I was seeing here. My father's car in Venezuela didn't have tinted windows like Antonio's car did. It made me nervous as the car inched down the street and I felt like people could see in. My father said it was better that they saw who we were than have to guess about who we weren't. I realized how right he was when we passed several make shift memorials on the side of the street for loved ones that had been lost in a shoot-out with police weeks before.

My father didn't drive into a garage, his driver pulled up as close as he could to my father's apartment building. The street the building was on was busy; men were standing around smoking and laughing with one another, immediately moving out of the way as my father stepped out of the car. I glanced around hesitantly before getting out of the car. No one looked like they were in a rush. The men on the street stood watching as I got out of the car. Despite the men standing around, my father grabbed my bag in one hand as if he didn't see them and my hand in his other and started walking toward his apartment building. I was careful not to look at anyone directly; some of them looked like they were ready to tear us apart for no reason at all. I told myself I was scared and being ridiculous. If my father wasn't scared about anything there was no reason for me to be scared either.

When we finally got to my father's apartment building, I practically flew through the revolving door, jumping in front of my father as if I had some kind of idea where we were going. My father glanced at me, raising his eyebrows as he followed me in. I looked back at him and the two of us smiled as we were greeted by a doorman. The doorman smiled as my father introduced us. The doorman was twice my father's size and his chest looked like it was made out of steel. He was nearly two heads taller than my father and his voice was so deep it made my body tremble. He was like no other doorman I imagined. He looked more like a larger version of Gilbert. Something told me that he just wasn't a doorman as I didn't notice him greeting any of the other people who were going in or out of the building.

"Don't worry, he knows who to let in and who not to let in." My father said as we got into the elevator and the doors closed.

Confusion overcame me when he leaned forward and pressed the button for the fourth floor. I had imagined him living at the top of this six story building. I felt like I didn't know what was going on. I expected my father to be living large and yet when the doors opened to his floor, there was nothing special about it. The hallway looked dull and it smelled musty. The dark brown carpet didn't help its appearance. We walked down a long hallway, past several other apartments. I could tell from the smells and noises inside that there were other families that lived there. I don't know why I had imagined that the entire floor was his, but I did.

I soon found out that the whole building was his, but his apartment wasn't anything more special than any of the apartments that we walked past. He said that he spent his money buying real estate in the area and that his real estate consisted mainly of apartment buildings such as this. His apartment was small and everything looked like it was cramped into the tiny rooms of the apartment. I felt bad in thinking this, but it was definitely not something that I would ever think about bragging about. From the way that Antonio and his family referred to him, I would have thought that my father had a flashier lifestyle than he did. My father led me to the room that I would be staying in and went to the kitchen to make something for us to eat.

I sighed as I settled in my make shift room. My view was of another apartment building and it was positioned so closely that I could smell the clean scent of the laundry that hung from one of the tenant's balconies, it lured me to it and I walked out onto the balcony to observe the area. There was nothing scenic about my view. From where I stood I could see the slums at the far west end of the city. I shook my head as I walked back inside my room. My father had obviously attempted to make the room comfortable for me, though it was apparent that he used it for work. Boxes with paper left behind and stacked up in my bedroom closet, making me curious what was on the paperwork inside them. There was a brand new bed in the room, still wrapped in plastic.

I smiled wondering if my father was planning to return it when I left. A bag at the end of the bed contained sheets and a pillow. I rustled through it as I sat on the bed. Shivering in delight to find that they were my favorite color, purple. It made me feel good to know that my father remembered that simple fact from our many conversations. Besides this, I couldn't help but to realize how cheap my father was as I looked around the room. From the way that he dressed, I would have thought that he lived very differently. The floors were made up of cheap vinyl tiles, the walls looked like they needed a coat of paint and the ceiling fan made a loud noise as it spun. Was I being materialistic, I wondered.

"Is everything okay?" My father's secretary came in and asked in a deep accent, after passing by in the hallway and seeing the horrified expression on my face.

I smiled and nodded as I stared at her. She was my father's age, but she was beautiful. Her hair was long and black, she wore a skirt to her knees with a dressy pink blouse and red sequined scarf. Her extreme sense of style floored me. She looked like she didn't belong in this drab apartment but on the front cover of a magazine. I could tell from the way that she watched me she had deep feelings for my father. There was a long while that she stood there, without saying a word. She smiled bleakly and I wondered if she was analyzing me, just as I was doing with her.

"Do you need anything from the store?" She finally asked. "I need to pick up a few things.

"Actually would you mind if I go with you." I asked, standing up quickly from the bed.

It was the middle of the day and I didn't have any idea what I'd do at the house all day. Somehow the way she looked at me made me feel safe in going with her, in spite of how scary the streets were. I told myself that regardless of the fact that I was scared to hit the city streets, I wanted to see all that Venezuela had to offer me while I was there. I followed her out of the room and my father smiled as he began to chop vegetables as he prepared dinner.

"I see that you've met my lovely assistant Alejandra." My father said as he stared at us.

Alejandra smiled and gave him a seductive look, waving at my father as I tagged along behind her.

"Do you have your card with you?" My father asked.

Alejandra nodded at him and grabbed my hand leading me out the door. She seemed to be on a mission and I went along with it.

Chapter Nine

The next morning, I woke up with every bone in my body aching. Alejandra and I had taken a taxi to a shopping district and then walked to several different stores in town. We didn't stop there, she even took me to see a few area attractions and we stopped for ice cream before coming back home. I was in shock as we sat down at an ice cream stop and ten kids came to us, trying to sell us candy. Alejandra bought one for each child and even purchased an ice cream cone for each one of them. She was so nice to each of them that it amazed me that she had never had children of her own. I was surprised that my father wasn't upset that we showed up late for dinner. He greeted us both and rushed to heat up the food as soon as we got back to the apartment.

"Tomorrow we'll ride the cable car to the top of Mount Avila." Alejandra told my father and me over dinner.

I laughed out loud. She had mentioned it earlier and there was no way that I was taking that ride. I was scared to death of heights, though I hadn't mentioned it to either one of them yet. I sat up in my bed abruptly, remembering that Antonio had called the night before while we had that conversation. I had avoided his call, telling Alejandra and my father about our current situation, though I wasn't sure if she understood me or not. I had forgotten to tell either of them that Antonio didn't know I was here and I knew if Antonio tried to reach me again and I didn't answer he would be calling the house and a maid was sure to tell him that I had left with my father and not come back.

I quickly got out of my bed and got dressed. The moment I walked into the living room, I saw Alejandra sitting at the desk in the living room not doing much of anything. Actually she didn't do too much aside from talking in a flirtatious matter with my father's guests. I excused myself going to the bathroom to take a shower. I quickly showered and dressed while in the bathroom, listening as I heard several different people come in and out of the apartment in the matter of the fifteen minutes that I was in there. A scruffy looking man was just leaving as I walked out to the living room; I shook my head and flung myself onto the sofa across from where Alejandra was. She smiled hesitantly and then went back to reading a magazine. My father called out to me, telling me that we would leave in the next half hour or so.

"Who was that leaving?" I asked.

My father shook his head and pretended like he didn't hear me.

"Did you want something to eat?" Alejandra asked.

"Sure." I replied.

"There is cereal in the top cabinet in the kitchen." She said.

I sat in shock momentarily before going to the kitchen. I hadn't had cereal in years. That just wasn't one of the things we ever ate at home, not even the kids had tried it. I didn't mean to look resentful as I walked past my father and into the kitchen to prepare myself something to eat. My father raised his eyebrows at me as I passed by him. I knew that he realized that I was used to being waited on hand and foot, but it was clear that wasn't happening in his house and I didn't mind. I looked down at my cell phone as I ate my cereal, noticing that I had just missed Antonio's call. It wouldn't be long until he found out where I was. I debated on calling him back before he called home, but decided against it. He was going to find out sooner or later, that I was in Venezuela I told myself.

When I was done eating my cereal I sat down nervously on my father's old maroon couch, and waited nervously for Antonio to call back. When he called back I told myself that I would not let him know how scared I was to be away from home. The night before, one of the neighbors in the apartment building across the way had been arguing loudly with his wife. Intrigued by their conversation I stepped out onto the balcony, only to see them inside their apartment, just as the husband slashed his wife's face with a razor blade. I immediately stepped back into my room and gasped as I made my way into the living room. I took one look at my father as he sat working at his desk with Alejandra and decided that scared or not, I was determined to stick it out and get to know my father. I quietly told him what I had seen and rather than calling the police, he said that he'd have his doorman go over and see what the problem was.

My father's phone rang as I sat there thinking about what had happened and it brought me back to reality. My father answered the phone, immediately walking across the room and handing it to me.

"Antonio." He said and walked back to his desk.

I slowly held the phone up to my ear, knowing what was coming. Before I could get a word in, Antonio started in, attempting to tear my head off over the phone. I held the phone away from my ear as I glanced over at Alejandra who could obviously hear him.

"Don't you know that Venezuela is one of the most dangerous places in the world?" Antonio screamed into the phone. "Do you think Chicago's bad? You don't know what you're getting yourself into there? Are you crazy? Your father is going to get you killed!"

I didn't say anything for a moment and then as calmly as possible, I responded.

"Antonio, sweetheart." I said quietly. "I don't know what I'm getting myself into at home either. Apparently it's also very dangerous there and who knows, I could get killed there just as easily."

He didn't wait for me to finish, he cut in before I could finish my sentence, I heard him screaming different rants, but with my final statement, I hung up the phone. My chest trembled in frustration.

"Princess, I'm sorry." My father said from across the room. "I thought he knew that you were here."

I shook my head and let out a small laugh, exchanging glances with Alejandra.

"No, actually I didn't tell anyone I was coming." I said softly.

I had already shared my story with Alejandra. She knew what was going on and the expression that she gave my father seemed to tell him to leave it alone. I had told her about all the grief that Antonio put me through, I wasn't sure that she understood everything I told her, but she nodded as I spoke to her and it honestly helped to have someone to talk to about my situation, even if she didn't understand. My father stared at me as if he wanted to say something, but simply shook his head and gave me a coy smile. I laughed as our eyes met and felt comfortable, knowing that whatever the situation may be, he was on my side.

His phone rang again, this time it was someone else and within seconds, he was lost in a quiet conversation. Caracas, the city my father lived in, was a big city with a great deal of crime. Antonio had good reason to be worried and he had warned me about it. I did however not feel that anything would happen while I was in my father's care, but boy was I wrong. Days later, on a visit with my cousins, I would find out just how dangerous the city was.

Chapter Ten

Two weeks later I freaked out about hearing gunshots while I was sleeping, followed by someone screaming at the top of their lungs for help. I ran out of my room and stood staring at my father. He looked up from the paperwork he was working on at his desk and Alejandra walked across the room to his side, both of them studying me to see what the problem was.

"Don't you hear that?" I asked.

Alejandra smiled and shook her head, going back to whatever it was that she was doing. I couldn't understand why neither of them seemed concerned, the screaming had yet to stop and it sounded like someone was in the process of dying.

"Liliana this is how life is here." My father said, noticing the terrified expression on my face. "There is nothing to worry about, this is completely normal."

"So just ignore it?" I responded.

He nodded his head and smiled lightly. I stared at him for a long while without saying a word. Eventually he stood up and came over to me, kissing me on my head, before walking off to his bedroom.

"I'm going to sleep." My father said. "I suggest you do the same."

I stared at the living room window intently, wondering how anyone could accept chaos as their way of life. If I had to raise my children here, I would be constantly worried.

"Shouldn't we call someone?" I asked.

My father laughed.

"Alejandra." He called out.

She reluctantly stood up from the sofa.

"Will you call someone?" He asked.

"Who should I call?" Alejandra responded.

"Exactly." My father said. "Exactly."

He closed the door without saying another word. I stood completely still for a moment, staring at Alejandra. She watched me without saying a word. Rather than going back to sleep I walked into the living room. The apartment was so small that we were aware of where one another was at all times when we walked around the house. I wasn't sure if I even wanted to come back to Venezuela. How could I? I thought it over as I walked over and sat down on my father's couch and smiled to myself as I fell asleep.

Later that night I woke up to go to get a drink of water and quickly stood up, only to see Alejandra laying across the dining room table, with my father's head buried between her legs and the sides of her red satin robe hanging from either side of the table. Didn't they realize I had fallen asleep on the sofa I wondered? If they were an item, they should leave whatever they're desires were for the bedroom. Alejandra didn't move or push my father away as our eyes met from across the darkened room. My face began to burn and I realized that I had been standing there watching my father go at it for at least a minute. I excused myself and quickly went back to my room, shutting my door, my heart pounding heavily.

I touched the sides of my waist. I had never allowed Antonio to do that to me. It looked disgusting, but watching the two of them made me question how it would feel. Neither Alejandra nor my father came after me to explain, they didn't have to. They knew that I knew what they were doing and they seemed totally open about it since neither of them moved when I walked into the room. Moments later I heard Alejandra's muffled moans from the other room. I put my hand on my chest as I sat up on my bed to listen. I wasn't trying to eavesdrop, but I always tried to keep it quiet when Antonio and I were together. I suddenly wondered if he wished that I was louder. I debated on whether or not to walk out onto the balcony to watch them.

I laid back and pulled the blankets up to my shoulders to prevent myself from going to the balcony, but within seconds the moaning seemed to gain in intensity and I found myself getting out of my bed. I quietly tiptoed to the balcony door and shook my head as I turned and walked back to my bed, wondering what was wrong with me. This was my father, I thought, the thoughts that were going through my head disgusted me. Still I wondered how it was possible that he was still functional. I quickly lay back against my pillows and pressed my eyes tightly closed, trying to focus my attention on the noises from outside of the apartment.

Although we were on the fifth floor I could hear the faint voices of people talking either on the street or on their own balconies and then suddenly the sound of someone else in another apartment building having sex. Did no one sleep around here? I wondered. In the distance I could hear two people begin to scream at each other. They were so loud that I could hear their words pronounced with complete clarity. It was a husband and wife and before long he began to threaten her, saying that he was leaving and then a crashing noise echoed in the background. I jumped out of bed and walked over to my balcony, cracking the door slightly, so that I could hear them better.

"I'm going to kill her!" A man shouted at a woman two floors below our apartment in the building across the way.

"She has nothing to do with this." The woman retorted.

"She has everything to do with this." The man said loudly. "She's his daughter."

"Are you crazy? You'll be dead yourself in an hour." The wife shot back. "As if her father isn't bad enough. What do you think her husband will do?"

"I don't care." The man responded. "It will totally fulfill me to get revenge on El Jefe just one time. His actions have been affecting my whole life. Our lives!"

Did he just say my father's name, I wondered. I told myself that I must have heard him wrong.

"You know he doesn't care about anything." The woman responded. "His heart is stone. Look at what he did to me. How he left me."

"First of all, you're a whore if you thought he was going to be with you." The man shouted. "Secondly you are my woman, who told you to run off with him. What did he think he was going to do, ask you to marry him?"

"You said to do it! You wanted it just as bad as I did." The woman said. "If you would have fucked me once in a while this would have never happened Oswaldo! I would have never fallen for his moves. Anyway it would have benefited both of us if he married me. I would have a piece of his empire."

"You know him so well." The husband shot back, laughing loudly.

The woman remained quiet.

"If you hadn't slept with him, none of this would have happened." The husband said loudly after a moment's thought. "If you hadn't slept with him, my brother would still be alive."

I slowly climbed out onto the balcony and looked around cautiously, to find the apartment that the commotion was coming from. It was two buildings over and two floors down from where we were. I could see the woman's silhouette in the window.

"It's not my problem your brother went to him!" The woman shouted. "If you would have given me the attention that I needed, that I deserved, everything would be different."

The man didn't wait for her to finish.

"What attention?" The man shouted. "The man passes you on the street and pays you a compliment and days later you're in bed with him."

"It wasn't just any man." The woman said loudly. "He could have made us rich."

"Say what you want, I call that being a whore!" The man responded.

The woman slapped him hard. The echoing sound rippling down the street.

I covered my mouth in a giggle and stepped back.

"If you think that you were any more than a whore to 'El Jefe' you know as well as I do that you were wrong." The man screamed.

There it was, my confirmation. I saw the silhouette of the man as he left the apartment, slamming the door shut loud enough to cause more echoes to ripple through the street. Wait a minute, I thought to myself, he was talking about killing me. My hand remained over my mouth as I turned ever so slowly to my balcony door. I had to tell my father, I thought to myself and started toward the living room entrance, turning in that direction and catching a glimpse of Alejandra bent over the side of the sofa, with my father behind her, thrusting himself into her over and over again. Whatever they were doing didn't even look enjoyable as Alejandra's eyes seemed to bulge in pain. I couldn't help but stand there and watch the two of them, this time however I wasn't interested in seeing what they were doing, but trying to understand the man my father was.

Chapter Eleven

The following two weeks went by very slowly. I didn't know what to say to my father. He and Alejandra's relationship bothered me. When I told my father about what I heard at the balcony, he belittled the things that I told him. I went on to tell him that I had seen him and Alejandra going at it on two occasions and he laughed and tried to deny everything. Alejandra didn't look at me for a week and I had to tell my father that I would be cutting my visit short.

I didn't question her or any of them directly, but I questioned both of their morals. Alejandra was married, but spent the majority of her time with my father, she had for years. According to her, she found out her husband was in a relationship with someone else and never went back. I decided that if I stayed with my father I might end up either dead or in a relationship with someone else and I didn't want that. It was bad enough that Antonio had cheated on me several times; surprisingly I didn't have the desire to retaliate and get even with him by sleeping with anyone else. I decided that I had to get out of Venezuela. I wanted to be back with Antonio and my children.

In spite of everything that was going on, my father and I had spent a great deal of time together during the last two weeks. In that short amount of time that I was in Caracas, numerous men came to visit my father. Many of their appearances were scrubby and many of them looked scary. I often wondered if any of them were the man that I had overheard arguing with the woman on that scary night. When my father began to notice my anxiety he started going to meet each of them at the door, not letting them in. I could tell that they were up to no good and it made me nervous that all of these dangerous looking people knew where my father lived.

Alejandra seemed to be uncomfortable when he invited a select few of the men into the apartment and went out of her way to talk to me, so that I wouldn't notice whatever it was that they were doing in the other room of the apartment. I knew that there was something going on and although I didn't know what it was, I didn't want any part of it. I wanted to get out of Caracas as soon as possible, but the earliest available flight back to Colombia wasn't until Saturday.

My father had already paid for my ticket, regardless of the fact that he didn't want me to go. He pleaded with me to stay for a few more weeks, but I declined, bringing up the fact that he and Alejandra were welcome to come and visit me in Colombia any time. My father didn't like the idea, but he respected my desire to leave. Though his meetings with odd people didn't stop, he mentioned he wanted to take me to meet a few of my cousins that afternoon. Later that morning, Antonio called and I had a quiet conversation with him as my father entertained two of scrubby looking men in the kitchen.

When the phone rang, I immediately walked out onto the balcony, carefully shutting the door behind me. Alejandra glanced up and I smiled, thinking that I could whisper a few things to him without her noticing, shaking my head after a minute or so of him asking me to repeat myself and turned around and walked into my room through the adjoining door. I let out a big sigh when I was inside and thought that no one could hear me.

"I'm sorry," I said lightly. "It's so noisy outside."

"What's wrong beautiful?" Antonio asked. "It sounds like you have something on your mind."

I nodded my head in agreement, pausing briefly before saying anything. If he only knew how much I had on my mind. I glanced around my room, before beginning, making sure that my door was closed and that no one else could hear me.

"I do." I said quietly into the phone. "Antonio, I have to talk to you."

"What is it Lily?" I could sense the immediate concern in his voice.

"Antonio, I don't feel comfortable here anymore." I replied quietly, nearly breaking out into tears.

"Why, what did he do?" Antonio said loudly, his voice showing signs of anger. "I'll kill him if he did anything to hurt you."

I shook my head as if he could see me, desperately trying to control my voice as it fluctuated in intensity.

"It's not that." I replied. "He's been nothing but good to me."

"Then?" Antonio asked.

"Oh Tony," I said quietly, hearing my father's guests leaving. "I'll explain when I get back home."

"Tell me now." Antonio said. "Is everything okay?"

"Yes, everything is fine." I said. "I just want to go home. I'll tell you everything when I get there. I have to go now."

No Turning Back

I looked around the room nervously. I felt like someone was watching me and turned just as someone in the apartment building across the way, stepped back and out of view. I heard Antonio breathe deeply in frustration and I hit the end button on my phone and looking down at it and then around the room. I glanced outside at the building across the way and then ducked back as I noticed someone peer up at me. There was a knock at the door and I nearly jumped across my room. My father didn't wait for my reply, and let himself in with a quick shake of the door handle.

"Is everything alright, mija?" My father asked, noticing my frightened expression.

I sighed and glanced around the room at the walls.

"Do the decorations bother you in here?" My father asked.

I shrugged my shoulders and nodded my head, smiling lightly. He had posters of different types of guns lining the walls.

"I can have them moved to another room." My father said. "I'm just not used to having company stay over, aside from Alejandra."

"Dad, it's not a problem, really." I said hesitantly, grimacing at the thought of him and Alejandra. "I'm not sure that I'll be coming back here."

"What," my father looked shocked. "Why not?"

I shook my head, not wanting to speak for a moment, my hands beginning to shake. My father walked over to me and immediately sat down on the bed beside me. He looked at me, his expression questioning my response.

"Dad, I just feel safer at home." I replied. "This lifestyle of yours is too much for me. I know the things Antonio might do are not that much different, but I feel safe when I'm at home. I feel afraid here and I don't like to feel like that."

I studied his expression. I didn't want to hurt his feelings, but I wanted to be honest with him. I didn't want to come back here again, I felt like I was stupid to decide to come here in the first place. My father nodded his head. His face immediately showed signs of guilt. I let out a long sigh and smiled, attempting to make it better. I didn't want him to back away from me. I needed him in my life and wanted him in my life as my father. I couldn't help but question how that would be possible, given that he lived such a dangerous lifestyle.

"I understand." He said. "Well I can always come and visit you."

I laughed and nodded.

"Mija, I may not have the body guards or the visual wealth that Antonio has, but you are never in danger when you're with me." He laughed and seemed to go deep in thought.

"What is it?" I asked.

My father shook his head.

"I have an idea." He said, without smiling pulling out his cell phone and quickly beginning to dial numbers. The expression on his face scared me. When he looked up at me he instantly noticed the concern in my face and quickly changed the subject.

"Come on, let's go." He said. "I have a big surprise for you."

Chapter Twelve

I soon found out that his surprise was taking me to meet a few of my cousins at a festival. I hadn't dressed to be walking around and felt frustrated when I saw the enormous line we had to wait in, before even getting inside the gates. I was immediately aggravated with him and his decision to take me there.

At this point in our relationship the only person in my family that I wanted to get to know was him. I tried to persuade him to go elsewhere, but he said that it was important to him that I meet them before I head back home. Their mother was his closest sister and when I told him that I'd rather go and meet her, he seemed unconcerned. I stood sulking as sweat dripped from my body and he talked to various people that knew who he was.

The truth was that I was actually nervous to meet my cousins. I wondered what they would think of me. I stood completely still while I tried to convince myself that whatever they thought was unimportant to me.

"Do they even know we're coming? I asked as we waited for them to show up in the hot sun, the crowd inching toward the gate.

"This is my beautiful daughter." My father said, introducing me to several people, whom he went on to say that he had known for years.

"Mucho gusto." One said, shaking my hand as he exchanged an odd glance with my father.

My father went on to speak with them in Spanish as I stood uncomfortably watching them, slowly moving away from me as they spoke. I tried my best to understand what they were saying, but when I couldn't pick up on it, I dazed off. I thought about my boys and being at home with them. It had only been a little over a month since I'd seen them, but I knew they had probably done quite a bit of growing.

"Late again?" I heard my father suddenly exclaim and turned to see him shake his head in a joking manner.

I looked to my right and saw two girls who resembled me in appearance approaching us. I immediately felt even more out of place. It was apparent that both of them were very into fashion and I wouldn't doubt that they had also had work done. Their bodies were perfect and both of them were very busty.

"Tio." One said racing forward to embrace my father.

"It isn't easy looking this beautiful." The other said, smiling coyly at me as she waited her turn to hug him.

They then turned and smiled at me. I could tell immediately that I didn't like them. Something about them told me that they were putting on a show for me. My father turned and introduced me to my two cousins Zayelli and Nayeli quickly, before handing us each a wad of money and disappearing into the crowd. I stood with the money in hand in confusion, not knowing what had just happened. Did he think that I was a child? I debated on going after him. How was he going to leave me with these two girls who yes were my cousins, but I didn't know a thing about.

"Well aren't you lucky?" Zayelli said. "You get to spend the day with us. Don't worry, we'll teach you a thing or two to help you fit in around here."

"I wasn't actually worried about fitting in." I replied, fuming as I thought over what she had just said.

Nayeli snapped me out of my thought process by grabbing my hand and taking off, talking a mile a minute as we walked through the crowd. I soon learned that the two were identical twins, though they didn't look that much alike. They were nineteen years old, just a few years younger than me, yet they acted like they were at least ten years younger. They giggled at every male that walked by them and stopped to exchange phone numbers with several.

"It's just a game." Zayelli explained to me, eyeing my wedding ring as I watched her. "We'll throw them away later, besides I only date married men."

My eyes nearly popped out of my sockets. Had she sensed my awkwardness? I knew that she sensed my anxiety, from the way she laughed afterward. I stood up straight and eyed her in an attempt to show that I wasn't afraid of her. If this was what my cousins were like, I didn't want to have anything to do with them.

"Aye, Zayelli." Nayeli exclaimed. "Don't talk like that, you know Liliana is married."

Zayelli smiled slyly and winked her eye at her sister.

"And pregnant, I know. It's very obvious isn't it hermanita." Zayelli said. "I hear that he's cute, you better watch out prima."

I didn't know how to react to her. Nayeli stepped between us and shoved her sister.

"Stop it." Nayeli said to her sister, before turning to me. "She's only a few minutes older than me but she acts like its decades."

I wanted to punch Zayelli, but I could tell that she had just done it in order to get a reaction from me and I wasn't about to give it to her. When I said nothing, she glanced angrily at her sister.

"Fine. Let's go get some food." Zayelli said. "I would never even think about having kids, my vagina is too important to me."

I walked in shock, without being able to say anything.

"You have kids already?" Nayeli asked me.

"Yes, I have two twin boys." I said.

"Twins!" Zayelli exclaimed. "Your vagina must be humongous."

I stopped walking without saying a word, but Nayeli grabbed my arm and pulled me along. I felt beyond uncomfortable. Where did Zayelli get off saying things like that? It was apparent she didn't have respect for anyone. As we walked, we passed a group of girls dressed in colorful bikinis and feathered headdresses. I couldn't help turning my head to look at them. I hadn't quite figured this country out yet and I had no idea what was going on.

"I bet your husband would like that, huh?" Zayelli said. "I have one of those outfits at home. Can you imagine if Nayeli and I came over one day in them and paraded around your swimming pool?"

"Enough already Zayelli." Nayeli said, pausing as she noticed a group of men nearby.

"You do have a swimming pool, don't you?" Zayelli asked.

The men approached us, introducing themselves while Zayelli openly adjusted her bra. Leaning forward and laughing as if she hadn't just done it on purpose. I quietly backed away, putting my hand on my stomach as I did so, as a means of pointing out my pregnancy so that no one would attempt to approach me. I saw that one of the men wore a wedding ring and was not surprised when Zayelli went right for him, complimenting him on his pants and asking if she could touch the material. Before too long there were two men for each one of them and I was hanging back helplessly as I followed them around the festival, becoming more and more annoyed with my cousins and becoming more and more anxious to get away from them. After about five long minutes, I excused myself, breaking away from the crowd and walking toward the entrance of the park where there were tables set up and a band performing onstage. I sighed loudly as I fidgeted, trying to make myself comfortable on the steaming hot metal bench.

"What are you doing, sitting here alone?" A voice said.

I turned as a man sat down next to me. I shrugged and turned back to watch the performance.

"You think this is good?" The man said. "You should come back to see what goes on for Carnival Venezuela."

No Turning Back

I sat quietly for a moment and then turned back to the man.

"What goes on then?" I asked him hesitantly.

He laughed loudly, revealing a few missing teeth, his now noticeable stench revolting. He smelled like he had been drinking for days and at the same time never in his life used a toothbrush. I tried to avoid vomiting as my inquisitiveness turned to fear about what he would say or do next.

"A tourist huh?" He said loudly.

I looked away and noticed several people turn to glance at us. I had fallen into his trap.

"Not really." I said quietly, "Excuse me, I have to find my father."

I stood up, immediately hearing a huge commotion followed by, gunfire. Over ten shots were fired and I started to run in the same direction as everyone else, afraid because I couldn't run as fast and all but the elderly passing me by. I looked back and as the crowd loosened up, I turned and saw my father standing in the center of the sidewalk yelling at two men. There was a body lying on the ground, drenched in blood and my father turned a gun on the two men, shooting each of them at point blank range. I gasped as my run slowed to a walk and I walked backwards staring at him, afraid that I was going to fall over I finally stopped and watched as he put his gun away and turned to walk off as if nothing had happened. Four security guards stood nearby and nodded at him as he walked past them and I shook my head to make sure that I wasn't dreaming.

I couldn't believe what had just happened. I stood motionless and in complete shock for what felt like days as I watched him walking nonchalantly into the festival, toward the place I knew my cousins were. I slowly backed into a portable bathroom and reached into my pocket, realizing that nothing was in there. I remembered the man's knee brushing against me when he sat down, realizing that I had been pickpocketed. For a second I didn't know what to do, I didn't want to be stuck without being able to get back to his house. I quickly forced myself to follow my father, glancing over my shoulder as if I was doing something wrong and making sure that no one else was doing the same.

I was scared out of my mind. Too scared to vocalize a call out to stop him and get him to wait for me, so I followed discombobulated and wondering what I was doing. Within a minute he turned around and saw me. We both stopped walking and I gazed up at him, my face red and bearing signs of frustration. For a moment we stood staring at each other without saying a word.

"Come on princess, let's go get something to eat." He said, grabbing my hand.

I quickly pulled my hand back from him. I knew he realized that I had seen what happened but neither of us said a word about it.

"Dad, I want to go home." I said.

He smiled and held his hand out to me.

"Not to your home, I want to go back to Colombia." I said. "I might even want to go meet Antonio in Chicago."

My father's expression changed and he seemed upset for a moment, his eyes quickly changing to those of understanding and eventually he nodded at me.

No Turning Back

"I'm sorry you had to see that." He said.

I smiled lightly at him.

"Me too." I replied softly, as we turned and I allowed him to lead me out of the festival in silence.

Chapter Thirteen

By the time my father dropped me off at the airport, I was convinced that I wanted to join Antonio and my children in Chicago. The flight would take longer of course, but I needed to see my boys and to hold them or anyone in my arms to remind myself that I was human. I longed for someone's touch, particularly Antonio's. I never thought that I would think of being with him as safe, but at this moment his arms felt like the safest place in the world for me. I felt confused beyond belief as I sat on the flight to Florida, where I would take an adjoining flight to Chicago. I couldn't believe that I was walking away from my father, I was beside myself. Never in a million years would I have imagined that I would return willingly to Antonio.

I felt like he was the one person that I could discuss my feelings with but my mind raced as I thought over what I would say to him when I got off of the airplane. I knew that I had to let him know that things would never be the same between us. I was sure that he didn't expect them to be, I mean how could they be? He had killed my mother. I gazed around at the people on the airplane, attempting to focus on something other than my life. Everyone on the plane seemed serious as they sat up straight reading magazines or typing on their laptops. They appeared as if they had their lives in order, as if they had never experienced a problem as big as mine. I couldn't help wondering if they had.

No Turning Back

Hours before, I called Antonio to ask him to buy the tickets for me and to pick me up at the airport. He wanted to know what was going on but I told him that I would talk to him about it when I arrived in Chicago. My eyes had wondered outside to where I could still see my father's car sitting and waiting, perhaps wishing that I had changed my mind about going back home. I couldn't forget the expression that my father gave me as he dropped me off at the airport. My father had appeared overwhelmingly sad, but I knew as well as he did that he wasn't ready to be my dad.

My father was something else, he was offended that I wouldn't take his money to pay for the flight, but I couldn't do it and I didn't want him to know that I was going to Chicago. I didn't want to take anything else from him. I felt like he had done enough for me. I mean he had told me stories about my mother, that in my heart were sacred. Things that I would have never known if I hadn't come to stay with him in Venezuela, yet I felt like his money was dirty. I had no idea what he did to make it, but I knew that whatever it was and I didn't want to have anything to do with it. While Antonio wasn't legit either, I knew how much I missed my boys and that I couldn't go another day without being around them.

I sighed as I sat on the plane, thinking about everything that was going on in my life and reached down and dug my fingers into the sides of the armrest in anxiety. I felt like everything around me was going in slow motion, yet my mind was racing a mile a minute. I closed my eyes and tried to make myself fall asleep when I boarded the second plane to Chicago as it took off, but the passengers were noisy. Some of their conversations were so interesting that they wouldn't allow me to relax. By the time my plane prepared to land in Chicago, I realized that my life was about to change again and I was determined that this time I was the one who would be in control of it.

I could see Antonio standing nervously behind a glass wall, as I walked the ramp of the final steps leading to the airport. His expression showed that he did not know what to expect when I came to see him. I took a deep breath and cautiously walked around the corner of the ramp to meet him. He looked up, as if not knowing what to say. I wanted to remain angry, but couldn't, breaking into a smile as our eyes met. Immediately his troubled gaze disappeared, his lips parting into a wide grin. I raced through the crowd and threw myself into his arms.

He grasped me tightly and I could feel each of his fingers as he caressed my back, savoring every moment of his warm embrace and burying my face deep into his chest, wanting more than anything to be lost in this feeling forever. He smelled of men's cologne and I inhaled it as I ran my hands up his chiseled arms as I slowly pulled back and looked up at him. For a moment I didn't know if this was the right place to be, or the right feeling to have, but for now everything about my relationship with Antonio felt right.

He smiled as he pulled me back into him, stroking my back for several minutes as we stood in the middle of a crowded waiting area. I gazed out from him as he held me close, watching people rush past us to get to their luggage at the baggage claim and families that were sitting nearby, waiting patiently for the airplane to be cleared so that they could board their own flight. Antonio pulled back from me and looked down, biting his lip.

"It feels good to hold you Lily." Antonio said. "I've missed you so much."

I looked up and nodded at him.

"It feels good to be in your arms again." I replied, smiling and reaching up to stroke his face.

Antonio smiled and leaned down, passionately kissing me on the lips. I immediately felt warm and comfortable as he pulled me closer and closer to him. I was lost in his embrace and ran my hand down his back, pulling him closer to me. As we stood in a sensual lip lock, I realized that those around us were watching us and began to feel uncomfortable, opening one eye and noticing that people in the airport were walking by and smiling at us. I pulled away from him, blushing heavily and stood there watching him for a moment without saying a word. Antonio looked around and shook himself off, as if to show how intense our kiss had been.

"What happened with your father?" Antonio asked.

"Don't ask." I replied. "Not right now, just hold me."

Antonio smiled and pulled me into his arms, locking me in another tight embrace. We swayed back and forth for a moment, allowing me moments to think further into my relationship with him. Everything felt like it was right when I was with Antonio, I couldn't help the feelings that I had for him. Emotion went through my body, as I felt myself melt into his arms. I closed my eyes and imagined my mother looking down at me, frowning as she shook her head as if to scold me. I let out a heavy sigh as I pulled away from Antonio. I remembered what I told myself on the plane as I looked up into his dark brown eyes and reached up and rustled his hair to the side.

"I want you to know that nothing will ever be the same with us." I said softly as I stared at him. "I have to tell you that. You have to expect that things are going to be very different between us."

He pulled me close to him and pushed my head against his chest.

"I know." He said. "I know, mija. I am just so happy that you decided to join us here in Chicago and I promise you that this time I'm going to make everything right between us."

I sighed as he held me. These were things that I'd heard before, but I promised myself that this time I wouldn't let him or anyone else manipulate me ever again. I was going to prove everyone wrong when they thought of my as weak, but mainly I was going to prove my strength to myself and this was all part of it. This time I had a plan I thought, as I caressed his muscular arm. When we finally pulled away from each other, both of our eyes were watery. I clung tightly to his arm as we turned in the direction of a long white hallway and he led me to the baggage claim.

"You know Lily, I can't change the past." He said. "All that I can do is to ensure you a great future from this point on."

I nodded as I walked sadly beside him. My mind was already in other places as I looked around the airport. Each step was very difficult for me, because I knew if that last straw wouldn't have been pulled our life would be very different. If Antonio wouldn't have been the one who had killed my mother, I wouldn't feel guilty about being with him. The truth was that I didn't know if my life would have been better if I never had met him. Everyone's lives around me seemed to have their own set of problems, but if that night would have never happened, I wouldn't have the same family that I did today. Chicago would have been my home, I thought as I starred at the counter of a pizza place that advertised itself as having the world's best pizza. A line of people stood waiting patiently for the clerks to take their orders, as if the long wait was worth it.

No Turning Back

I sighed as I stared at two teenage girls who walked toward us, one holding a baby. Both of the girls had more makeup on than I had worn at my wedding. One complained to the other about how she wasn't able to go to school because her baby's daddy and his family wouldn't help her out. The girl couldn't have been older than fifteen. I stared at her for a moment as I wondered if her and her child's father were still together, realizing that if I had stayed here, my life may have not necessarily been better. I began to rethink my previous thoughts, remembering that God had a plan for everyone. I glanced at Antonio and smiled as the girls passed us.

"How's the baby?" Antonio suddenly asked, studying my reaction as he spoke. "Are you hungry?"

I smiled lightly and looked up at him. I put my hand on my stomach, shaking my head. I hadn't forgotten that I was pregnant, I just hadn't thought about it as much as I had with my last pregnancy.

"I guess everything is fine." I responded. "The baby moves around every once in a while."

Antonio grinned and hugged me again quickly, stopping as we walked and causing a group of people to nearly crash into us. Antonio apologized and led me on toward the baggage claim, laughing. We stopped in front of the conveyor belt and he pulled me close, wrapping his hands around my back and kissing me again passionately as we waited for my suitcase. His fingers stroked my back and my body shivered against his touch. I suddenly pushed him away and attempted to keep my composure as he was nearly caressing my buttocks.

"Are the kids back at the condo?" I asked nervously, removing his hands from my body as the crowd grew around us to gather their belongings.

Antonio nodded his head and looked away. I knew that he was having trouble controlling himself as he motioned for me to take a glimpse between the pockets of his pants. His pants were raised forward, as he tried to adjust himself by moving to different positions uncomfortably. I laughed and looked away, pointing out my suitcase as it approached on the conveyer belt and Antonio reached over and picked it up.

"Where's Gilbert?" I asked, suddenly realizing that he was missing.

Antonio grinned at me.

"He's with everyone else, downtown site-seeing." He replied.

My eyes grew large for a moment. Antonio hadn't made any major trips alone for as long as I had known him. He had told me on prior phone conversations that the condo was at least half an hour away from the airport. Antonio noticed my concern and grabbed my hand leading me to a set of glass doors, smiling all the while.

"Don't worry." He said in an attempt to ease my mind. "We don't need security here."

When we walked outside of the sliding glass doors of the airport, there was a line of taxi's waiting for customers. A cab driver got out of his cab and walked around the side, eying Antonio intently. Antonio nodded and the cabbie smiled, his whole attitude changing with the knowledge that we needed a ride. In that very instant, I realized how much everything had changed since I had lived here. Antonio led me to the taxi cab outside and the cabbie came around to put my suitcase in the back. I exchanged glances with Antonio as he opened the door for me and I slowly climbed in, watching him nervously as he walked around the side to sit down next to me.

"What's with the cab?" I whispered to Antonio as soon as he gave the cabbie directions to the condo.

"Everyone here rides in cabs, Lily." Antonio said while stroking my hand. "We're just blending in."

I glanced at him suspiciously, assuming he was at least halfway correct as I turned to stare out the window at the line of cabs waiting outside the airport. I felt anxious as Antonio gave the cab driver the address. I sat quietly trying to remember my old address and hoped that we would pass a sign leading to my old neighborhood. I leaned forward and asked the cab driver if he knew where my old address was, suddenly remembering it and he responded only that it was on the other side of town and asked if I knew someone in that area. I quietly shook my head and sat back without saying a word. Antonio stared at me momentarily as if he wanted to say something but didn't utter a word.

I thought of my Aunt and of all of her children. I wondered how big the kids were now and what they looked like. I wondered if my aunt would want to see me now, since I was no longer technically her niece. I sighed lightly as I looked out the window deep in thought. Antonio leaned in, as if he sensed my anxiety, and began pointing out different buildings out as the cab flew by them, wrapping his strong arm around my shoulder and pulling me close, tussling my hair with his nose. His efforts worked as I stopped worrying about my aunt and what my life had been for a moment and started focusing on the scenery.

Even leaving the airport, I was amazed by the city that I had been away from for so long. The names of major corporations lined buildings along our drive. As a young girl when leaving the city, the names of the buildings were not something that I had ever focused on before. While Colombia had areas that were heavily populated, they didn't come close to looking like this! How I missed being in a real city, where there was building after building and store after store along either side of the highway. I remembered my mother dragging me all around the city as a little girl. Shopping at various department stores that were like no other that I had seen in Colombia. The only thing that I didn't remember about Chicago from looking at the sides of the towering buildings was how dirty the city looked.

Our cab driver suddenly went from a good rate of speed to a complete halt. I put my hand to my chest and glanced at Antonio nervously, gripping his arm to avoid being flung into the seat in front of me. Antonio smiled as I was suddenly brought back to reality. I glanced out the front window to a line of cars stopped ahead of us.

"Traffic." Antonio said knowledgably, "You do remember the traffic here, don't you. Everywhere we go it seems to be stop and go."

I bit down on my lip. I couldn't say that I did remember the traffic being this heavy or this scary. I glanced around us as I noticed drivers attempt to change lanes and nearly get side swiped. Antonio smiled at my aggravation.

"Is it like this every day here?" Antonio leaned forward and asked the driver.

"Yes." The driver said with a heavy accent. "Every day, at this time of day anyway."

No Turning Back

I saw the driver glance back at us in his rearview mirror. I smiled lightly at him.

"It's kind of dangerous to drive here, isn't it?" I asked pointing at the front window. "I'm surprised that red car didn't get in an accident just now."

The cabbie glanced out the window for a moment.

"Where are you two from?" The cabbie asked.

"Colombia." Antonio said. "But I went to school here. In Indiana actually."

The driver smiled at Antonio and me through the mirror.

"Colombia huh?" The cabbie asked. "Everyone here will assume you're a drug dealer. Everyone here assumes I'm a terrorist."

Antonio laughed, as I sat in shock.

"Indiana is a nice place." The cabbie said. "No traffic there."

"Well less than here probably." Antonio responded. "She's actually originally from here."

Antonio nodded at me.

"My wife is." Antonio said. "She grew up here until she was a teenager."

"What area?" The cabbie asked. "The one you mentioned?"

I blanked out for a moment.

"I don't remember the neighborhood, just the address I gave you." I finally said. "My mother and I moved around a lot, that was our last address. I just went pretty much, wherever she took me."

"Oh." The cabbie replied. "What made you want to move to Colombia?"

"My mother died." I replied.

"That's terrible." The cabbie muttered, turning his focus to the road.

I bit my bottom lip again as I glanced out the window.

"I have a neighbor down the hall from me who is from Colombia." The cab driver said. "Maybe you know him."

Antonio laughed nervously.

"Oh, we come from a small town." Antonio quickly replied. "I can guarantee that your neighbor would have never heard of us. Colombia is a much bigger country than you might think."

"Eh, I guess you're right." The cab driver responded quickly.

At that moment the car behind us began to blare his horn at the cabbie.

"What, he moved an inch? You expect me to waste my gas for an inch." The cab driver screamed, sticking his head out of the window.

The car behind him continued to beep his horn until the cabbie moved the taxi cab forward slightly.

"Some people." The cab driver muttered under his breath and reached down to turn the radio on.

Antonio and I glanced at each other and smiled. Antonio began to talk to me directly about various things the family had done while they were in Chicago and as he spoke, I found myself listening to less and less of what he was saying, only to find myself paying close attention to the traffic and our cab drivers driving as the driver began to move the car to the side of another car, so close that we were almost touching them. I gripped Antonio's leg tightly after the cab driver suddenly switched lanes and turned to his side to give the car that was behind us the finger as he drove past. I gasped in shock and Antonio continued talking as if nothing had happened, rattling on and on about nonsense. I exhaled quietly as I sank as deep as possible into my seat, suddenly beginning to fear for my life as we sat stuck on a highway with four lanes of traffic going in each direction that was completely stopped aside from the car behind us who was playing stop and go and successfully making his way through traffic.

"So tell me about your trip." Antonio said, squeezing my hand as we sat motionless in traffic.

I let out a long sigh.

"What is there to tell?" I asked. "You know who my father is. Everybody does right?"

I stared directly at him and rolled my eyes. Antonio smiled and sat up straight.

"He called about an hour ago Lily." Antonio said. "He's worried about how you might feel toward him. He didn't tell me what happened, only that you had seen something that might have scared you."

Antonio stared at me intently, waiting for an answer. How was I supposed to respond to that, I wondered? In the short time that I had known him, my father showed me two very different sides of himself. I didn't know how to react to him or what to think about his lifestyle. I glanced away from Antonio's inquisitive expression.

"I don't know." I said quietly staring out the window. "I really just wanted to find out who I was. I wanted to understand where I belong and how my life falls into place in this crazy world that we live in."

I turned and looked deep into Antonio's eyes.

"Now I feel more confused than ever." I said lightly. "I feel lost and like I don't belong."

"You might think that you don't know who you are Lily." Antonio said convincingly, returning my helpless gaze, "I think it's just that you don't realize who you are. Deep inside Lily, you know."

I turned away.

"Hey look at me." Antonio said.

I turned toward him, my eyes beginning to burn from anxiety.

"Who I am and who your father is doesn't have anything to do with who you are." Antonio continued. "You're your own person and you're going to figure it out. I promise you that."

He broke into a grin as he stared at me. This time, the sexy way his curls hung over his face didn't make a difference to me.

Antonio started to speak again, but I immediately cut him off.

"I wish that I could believe you when you told me that everything was going to be alright and that everything was going to work itself out, but I can't." I said.

"Why mi Amor?" Antonio said, touching his chest. "I don't make you who you are. I am not the one who can make everything ok. Don't you get it? You are. It's not about believing me, it's about believing in yourself."

Antonio turned his body away from the cab driver, blocking him from my view and stared directly into my eyes, as if his shoulders acted as a barrier between our conversation and the driver and the traffic.

"Sweetheart, life is too short for spending it trying to figure things out." Antonio said, touching my chin softly. "You keep worrying about who you are and everything is just going to keep moving around you. Nothing is going to stop, the kids are going to grow up and you're still going to be searching for an answer to something that just can't be answered."

I turned away.

"I get it Lily. I don't mean to be a dick, I really don't, but I get it." Antonio went on. "Your mothers dead, your dad's cousin, who you thought was your father was and still is an asshole. Probably one of the biggest assholes in all of Colombia."

Antonio looked away briefly, before turning back to me.

"I've made my mistakes. I know, I have." Antonio said lightly. "Your father is still living on the edge, twenty something years later and there's nothing you or anyone could do about that."

He paused, as if to see if I was still paying attention to him.

"But we don't make you." Antonio said. "You're a big girl Lily. You'll always be my baby and I'm here for you, to help you and to be the part of a life that I can't live without you."

Antonio leaned in and said directly to me.

"It's time to grow up sweetheart." Antonio said, his gaze penetrating me. "You know who Liliana is. Now it's time for you to show the rest of us the person we have yet to know."

Chapter Fourteen

The next morning I woke up covered by rose colored silky satin sheets, as sunlight gleamed in from a window nearby. I felt like the sun was right outside of our window and I rolled over and put my arm around Antonio's muscular chest as he slept beside me. We had come straight back to the condo the night before and I hadn't had a chance to see the twins yet. Antonio took me downtown, when we arrived in the late afternoon but when we tried to catch up with the rest of the family, our cell phone reception was lost and we couldn't find them. We played phone tag for an hour and left a message that we would be eating dinner at a restaurant, but after a few glasses of wine, Antonio and I left and headed back to the condo, going on to have the best sex that we had ever had for hours on end.

Antonio opened his eyes and smiled at me, as he looked over at me.

"Let's get ready." He said softly. "I have to show you something."

"Where are the boys?" I asked. "I have to see them."

Antonio smiled and shook his head, his curls falling perfectly into place.

"They're gone already." Antonio said. "The nanny took them to the condo's kiddie gym."

I bit my lip and stared at him.

"What?" I exclaimed in shock. "Where's everyone else?"

"They're off enjoying the day." Antonio said smiling. "I told them we had plans."

When Antonio noticed my confused expression he immediately put his arm around me and pulled me close.

"I woke up at four, had some coffee, hung out with the family," He explained, as he positioned himself upright in the bed. "They were waiting around to say hello, but then it dawned on me that I had to take you somewhere very special. I let them know and after they left around eight, I came back to sleep with you. You'll see everyone tonight I promise, for now get dressed and let's get this day started."

Antonio climbed out of bed and slipped on a pair of fitted boxer shorts and stretched as he stood at the side of the bed, his muscles flexing as he did so, his fitted boxer short clinging to his buttocks. I smiled as I stared at his tan physique, reluctantly slipping on my own panties while staring at him. The sun glistened off his body as he stood there and I couldn't help but keep staring at him, rather than to move and begin getting dressed.

When he turned to look at me I didn't look away. Within seconds he was back in bed, seconds later he was on top of me, and seconds after that my panties were off. He teased me for a while before slipping his manhood into me. I wrapped my arms around his neck and clenched my teeth together as he began to penetrate me, I thought of Alejandra and my father and began to moan loudly, rather than to try to stay quiet as I usually did. At first he paused, seemingly surprised and then started up again, going harder and faster than he did before. I moaned the entire time we made love, even though some of my sounds became forced. I couldn't help myself as I noticed him smile in satisfaction as he thrust himself into me time and time again, causing me to feel hot and wet as I grabbed him and dug my nails into his back. When he was done, we both lay completely still in the bed for at least a minute.

"And I thought last night was good." I muttered as I felt my reflexes still tingling in delight.

"Come on, let's get ready." Antonio said, suddenly jumping up and rushing to the bathroom without looking back.

I laughed as I pulled the sheets up to my chest, sitting straight up on the bed and pulling my hair into a ponytail with a rubber band on the table by the bed. Within seconds I heard the water turn on and him begin to sing in Spanish. I stood up and walked around the room to my suitcase as I walked toward it, I noticed a full length mirror on the wall and paused as I stood completely naked before it. My stomach was not very big for being as pregnant as I was, but my stretch marks from the twins looked so much darker to me, than I had thought they were. I put my hand to them, feeling their deep texture as I ran my hand over them and glanced to the side to see Antonio lathering up his body from inside of the shower as he sang away.

I ran my hand over my stomach and looked down at it. Although my stretch marks were not quite as visible to me, I wondered if they were as visible as they showed in the mirror to everyone else. I became lost in thought as I stood there, running my fingers over my stomach and thighs, where I noticed the most stretch marks. *Was this how everyone else saw me*, I wondered. I suddenly leaned forward and looked at my breasts. They were huge, but not sexy at all, and covered with more stretch marks. I immediately covered them and stormed into the bathroom.

"Antonio." I whined as I walked in.

He leaned back and turned to me as he rinsed the soap from his body.

"Yes, my love?" He asked, leaning back to see what was going on.

"Look at me." I stammered. "How can you see me like this and not be disgusted?"

Antonio turned off the water and stepped out of the shower. His naked body appeared more toned and fit to me than it had minutes ago. I felt embarrassed as I stood there, confident only that I was the most disgusting looking woman on the planet. He stood drying his hair completely naked otherwise for a moment, before wrapping the towel around his waist.

"What are you talking about Lily?" He asked.

"These!" I exclaimed grabbing my breasts. "I have stretch marks all over the place, but here they look disgusting."

Antonio laughed as he walked past me in the small bathroom.

"I don't know what you're talking about." He said.

"Antonio." I whined as I turned to look at him, pointing out the stretch marks.

"So you have stripes." He said, turning his lip up. "You're like a tiger, big deal. I should be the one who's complaining, your cat like features just caused you to claw the heck out of my back. Do you have any idea how that felt in the shower?"

I smirked and spun around, climbing into the shower, feeling devastated with my appearance, and rushing myself to finish so that I could get my clothes on. An hour later, we headed across town to have breakfast.

"Did you think about what I said?" He asked as we sat down in a small restaurant and prepared ourselves to order.

"About what?" I asked as I studied the menu.

Antonio put his menu down and stared over the table at me.

"About figuring out who you are." He replied.

I sighed as I put my menu down, deciding just to eat whatever it was that he decided to order. I was completely stressed out by what he had just said. Was he joking? He had just told me yesterday that I was the only one who could figure out who I was. I debated on arguing with him, but it seemed like his intentions were good, and it seemed the harder I pushed to figure out who I was, the further away I got from figuring it out. I shook my head as I stared deep into his brown eyes.

"I don't know Antonio." I finally answered him. "I'm not sure I'm ever going to figure it out."

Antonio smiled as he stared at me. The waitress came to the table and took our order as I glanced around the restaurant. The only thing I had on my mind at this point was if one of the young men that was sitting waiting for their breakfast sitting alone, as if he would be going off to work soon could be one of my cousins.

I looked up but Antonio said nothing as he gazed off into the distance. Not even five minutes passed before our waitress arrived at our table with two plates of food and I wasn't positive but it looked like she was chomping on a massive piece of gum.

"Did they even cook it?" Antonio asked, smirking at me.

I smiled as I looked down at my plate and reluctantly began to eat. I wondered what had made Antonio pick this particular restaurant. This place wasn't the type of place Antonio would normally enjoy, I thought to myself. I felt nervous as we sat eating our food even though it was broad daylight. We were in what looked like a pretty rough neighborhood and the food looked like it was cooked in grease that had been reused at least four times. To top it all off, we had driven in heavy traffic for at least twenty minutes to get here, passing at least ten other restaurants that looked much more appetizing. I took a bite of food and tried my best to chew it. It actually wasn't half bad, but extremely greasy. I spent the next five minutes, picking at my food. The moment he was done, Antonio left some money on the table and then led me out, walking down a busy street nearby.

"Where are we going?" I asked.

Antonio reluctantly smiled.

"You'll see." He said under his breath as we walked.

I looked around nervously as he held me by the hand. Stores lined the street but we were beginning to get to a point that there would be nothing but apartment buildings. I looked at a tall red brick building nearby and my heart literally skipped a beat. I couldn't imagine who would want to live here, yet it was apparent that there were a lot of people who did live in the neighborhood. The neighborhood was a mess; trash overloaded garbage cans and seemed to spill out onto the street. Two minutes later and he completely stopped, looking around at the intersection and nervously smiling at me.

"Where are we Antonio?" I asked.

Cars sped past us, trying to avoid catching a red light and Antonio said nothing as we stood there. I looked around at the apartment buildings as Antonio stood silently watching me.

"Did you think about my question?" Antonio asked as he stared at me in the sunlight.

I squinted my eyes as I stared at him in confusion. He smiled nervously and moved his chin as if to point down the street at an alley, causing my heart to skip a beat. I knew where we were and tears began to fall from my face.

"Where are we Antonio?" I sobbed, as if I needed him to answer my question.

He said nothing, instead he pulled me towards him and I buried my head in the wool of his sweater as he rubbed my back to comfort me. People walked by us as I stood balling my eyes out on the street corner, giving us odd glances as they passed by. My tears dissipating after what felt like several minutes, I looked up at him. I knew where we were and I knew why he brought me here. This was the place that I had lost myself the day he killed my mother.

Chapter Fifteen

Two weeks later, I knew what I needed to do. I figured it out as we drove past Truman College on Wilson Avenue, headed west as we left our Condo on Marine Drive in an effort to make it to Old Orchard Shopping mall before they closed for the evening. We hadn't decided to leave at the best time and Elena apologized to Antonio repeatedly when our car became stuck in evening rush hour traffic.

For the longest time we were stuck at the corner of Wilson and Broadway, near a coffee shop and apparently not the best area to get stuck in. One man stood holding a sign that said "Homeless Please Help." He walked right up to the car with his sign and stood there, staring at us with puppy dog eyes until Miguel finally rolled down the window and handed him a twenty dollar bill, causing an uproar inside the car. Antonio yelled at him for doing it, he said it would only go toward helping him with whatever bad habit he had. I looked away and stared down the street, positive that he was right. Several men sat at a bus stop nearby, drinking out of brown paper bags and holding signs of their own as they talked amongst each other.

Several minutes later we inched west on Wilson Avenue, under a viaduct that an "El" train, passed over at an overwhelming decibel. As I sat there watching the train pass, I noticed a college on the left-hand side of the street and also noticed that the delay in traffic was due to two fire engines, attempting to park, while cars passing were not offering them room to do so in spite of two firemen who stood outside, attempting to halt traffic. I turned away and stared not at the commotion in the street, but at the college in the midst of all this mess. I squeezed Elena's hand as I looked out at it. I saw people rushing into the building, books in hand and others talking with friends outside, as if deep in conversation about their classes. Elena glanced at me, noticing my attention was on the school.

"Elena, that's it." I said quietly. "I want to go back to school."

Elena raised her eyebrows at me and looked at the school. Antonio lowered the radio as he eavesdropped on our conversation. My eyes gleamed as I sat staring at the college, smiling and motioning with my chin to Antonio who turned and looked at the school. I was amazed, even more so seconds later when a woman came out of the school holding her daughters hand, her attention focused on paperwork that she held tightly so that the wind wouldn't blow it away.

"You know, some people in the United States get their high school diploma online now?" Antonio stated loudly. "You could do that."

Miguel and Elena glanced at each other as if both had just realized what was on Antonio and my mind. Suddenly our car picked up speed as the fire truck backed in the last few feet and traffic began to move again. I sat up straight, looking back as we passed the school. I couldn't help it. I was intrigued by my surroundings. I remembered that my mother had gone back for her GED when I was about six years old and I remember her telling me that she wished that she had received her high school diploma instead.

Hours later as Elena and I went through racks of clothing, my attention was focused elsewhere. Antonio and Miguel headed off to a pizza place, leaving us to search for clothing for the kids, as Chicago's weather had suddenly taken a turn toward cold weather. We would meet them when we were done and rather than me getting any shopping done, I leafed through clothing racks, without thinking about clothes, only on the girl that I had seen holding her mother's hand instead of on and what looked nice and what didn't.

"Lily, what do you think?" Elena called across a clothing rack, holding up an outfit.

I nodded my head nonchalantly and smiled in approval. Elena pursed her lips together as if she was annoyed with me.

"Why are you so quiet today?" Elena asked.

I shook my head and shrugged my shoulders, smiling.

"I have other things on my mind, I guess." I responded.

Elena looked down at the clothes in her hand and immediately laid them over the side of a rack.

"You aren't thinking about going back to school, are you?" Elena asked.

I nodded and smiled at her.

"What do you think?" I asked, grabbing her hand. "My cousins I met were so intelligent. I want to be like that. I want to show my kids that I have a future outside of my life with Antonio."

Elena frowned disapprovingly.

"What about the kids?" Elena asked. "What are they going to do while you're taking classes?"

I frowned at her.

"Elena, we have a nanny." I exclaimed.

She frowned harder.

"Did you hear Antonio mention that I could take the classes online?" I asked her, upset that she wasn't seeing the good in me going back to school.

"Lily, you don't even know how to turn on the computer!" Elena exclaimed. "How are you going to take classes online?"

I sighed.

"Don't discourage me Elena." I said. "Antonio will show me how to use the computer, I spend plenty of time doing absolutely nothing around the house, and this could be a great opportunity for me. Why don't you see that?"

Elena crossed her arms against her chest.

"An opportunity for what?" Elena asked. "Antonio can give you anything that you possibly need. I just don't understand what the point is."

I frowned at her and crossed my own arms against my chest.

"I don't want him to give me everything I need." I replied. "I want to be able to rely on myself. I'm sure that both he and my father could provide me with, whatever I ask them for, but don't you see? I don't want to have to ask anyone for anything."

Elena stared at me with a blank expression. I studied her face for a moment.

"I don't want to ask them for anything." I said abruptly, walking around the clothing rack. "I want to start doing things on my own."

I took a step toward her and put a hand on either of her shoulders.

"Don't you see?" I asked. "This is an opportunity for me to better myself. To become my own person and to be whoever it is that I want to be."

She nodded, but continued frowning as she stared at me.

"It's an opportunity for me to find myself without depending on anyone else for assistance." I continued, wanting ever so badly for Elena to break out into a smile.

Elena stepped back and laid her arms at either side for a moment, before crossing them again.

"And what about my brother?" Elena asked. "Is this an opportunity for you to get away from him? Are you planning on leaving him or the rest of your family?"

I turned around without taking a step away from her, feeling as if she had slapped me with her words and I let out a sigh and putting my hands to my head.

"I don't know." I said thoughtfully. "I don't know what is going to come of this. I mean I know that he didn't mean for any of this to happen and I don't want my family to fall apart, but right now this has nothing to do with Antonio and I, this is for me Elena. Don't you get it?"

I looked at her, my head tilted slightly as I stared into her eyes.

"I can't take the chance of being unprepared for tomorrow." I explained. "What if my father disappears? What if Antonio and the rest of you disappear, where does that leave me?"

Elena continued to eye me sternly.

"What about the twins?" I asked. "What about the baby?"

I held my stomach with both hands, as if to remind her that I was pregnant. She shook her head as she stared at me.

"Nothing like that is ever going to happen." Elena said. "You have Antonio and you have me as well as the rest of my family. They are your family Liliana."

I paced the floor and took a step toward her, putting my hand on my chest as I spoke.

"Yes but I want to be able to rely on myself." I said. "Don't you think that it will be beneficial not only to myself, but to the entire family if I go back to high school and later get a degree."

"What will you do with it?" Elena shot back. "What will you go to school for?"

I noticed the heads of the store clerks turn as we stood in the middle of the store having our discussion. My face flushed with embarrassment.

"I don't know, maybe I could learn to manage money." I replied firmly. "It might take a while to figure it out, but I need to do it. Can you imagine the position the entire family would be in if I learned to double our money legally."

Elena's expression was unchanged. Her eyes were full of curiosity, but she still seemed upset about my decision.

"Why can't you support me on this?" I asked, picking up her pile of clothes and taking it to the register.

The clerk rang up the clothes and raised her eyebrows at the girl who stood next to her bagging them up, when I pulled out the wad of cash that Antonio had given me.

"Were you interested in one of these wallets, with your purchase today?" The clerk asked me lightly, motioning to wallets that lined the register.

I shook my head and took my change back from her.

I felt someone put their arm around my shoulder and turned to see Elena, her eyes full of tears.

"I support you Lily, ok I do." Elena said, immediately hugging me.

I wrapped my arms around her, change still in hand.

"I just don't want you to ever think about leaving my brother, because that would mean that you were leaving my family." Elena said, sniffing. "And leaving me. I don't want you to ever do that."

I rubbed her back as we held each other in front of the store clerks. I felt slightly awkward as we stood there, and was appreciative that we were the only customers in the store.

Chapter Sixteen

Months later and back home in Colombia, I sat brushing my hair, reminiscing on the time that we spent in Chicago. It was difficult for me to go back to loving Antonio the same way that I had, and although I could never forget what Antonio had done, I realized that in order to continue with our relationship, I needed to find a way to forgive him. Any time bad memories entered my mind, I did my best to push them out. The more I did this, what he had done didn't bother me as much and I found myself thinking about the entire situation less and less.

Antonio and my relationship in the bedroom had grown steamier then ever since we returned from the United States. We made hot and passionate love at least three times a day, in spite of my protruding belly. We found out that I would be having another boy in the spring and I decided that I was going to have a surgery to avoid having any more kids when the baby was born, so that we would be able to keep our sultry sex life going without any surprises. While I had hoped that this baby was a girl, I decided to focus on getting my education rather than to have any more children.

"Senora." The maid called suddenly from behind my closed bedroom door, bringing me back to reality.

"Entrar." I called out to her, quickly putting my brush down and standing up to walk toward the door.

"Tu padre está aquí." She said quietly, her eyes glancing about the room nervously.

"Mi Padre?" I asked, wondering why my father had showed up at my house without calling first.

She nodded her head as she stared at me for guidance. I nodded at her and walked toward my bedroom door in confusion. She seemed hesitant as she led me down the stairs and her reluctance began to make me nervous. I felt as if something in the air had just overcome both of us. She motioned to the window when we arrived at the bottom of the stairs and I went over to look out. My father had brought Alejandra, she stood leaning against the car with her arms folded across her chest as if she was upset. My father looked like he was upset with her and when he saw me at the window, quickly ordered her to stand up straight, walking toward the front door to meet me.

I sighed heavily before going outside; I could tell that there was something concerning him. The moment I came outside he put his arm around my shoulders and led me away, to the bench we always sat down at when he came to visit. Alejandra greeted me but then proceeded to return to a sulking position against the car as she stood waiting for him to return, which I thought to be odd. Antonio, who was meeting with his relatives in the backyard stopped what he was doing and waved, while looking at me disapprovingly as my unannounced father sat down with me and quickly leaned in, as if he had something really important to talk about.

"You know your guards checked me before I came in. My entire car." My father said, laughing. "Do they think because Antonio is here with his family I am planning to do something to them? I was just in the neighborhood, so I decided to drop in."

I scowled at him, as he smiled at his secretary who stood in the distance.

"You are never 'just in the neighborhood', Papi." I replied. "Tell me the truth. What is going on?"

My father nervously fidgeted in his seat.

"What, a father can't come to visit his only daughter unannounced?" My father asked.

I glared at him and shook my head as I waited for an answer. Birds swooped down to play in the birdbath that was not far away from where we were seated.

"Come on, Papi." I said after several minutes. "Tell me what is going on."

He motioned for Alejandra to come over and join us and she reluctantly began toward us. Commotion broke out between Antonio and his family and within seconds, three of his cousins stood up and began to storm off to their cars. Tires flared against the pavement as they drove off. Alejandra paused momentarily before continuing to walk toward us. I glanced at Antonio who was a good distance away from us and gave him an apologetic look. He shook his head as he glared at my father. Alejandra glanced at me as my father motioned for her to sit down next to him. I became agitated as I sat waiting for either of them to begin talking. I raised my eyebrows at them as if to invite them to begin doing so.

"There's no easy way to say this." My father said. "Why don't you tell her Alejandra?"

My aggravation began to show as I began to twitch my right leg, which was crossed over my left one. Alejandra leaned forward and put her hand on my knee as she began to speak, her fingers nervously shaking.

"I'm pregnant." She said.

My expression didn't change. I was used to surprises and this wasn't a surprise to me, especially considering what I had seen at my father's house.

"Congratulations." I said, immediately glancing at my father and seeing from his expression that there was more to come.

My father shook his head as he studied my reaction, almost as if he was expecting more from me.

"It's you father's baby." Alejandra said.

"I kind of figured." I said plainly. "Why does it feel like there is more that you're waiting to tell me?"

"Liliana, I can't raise a baby." My father said briskly. "Alejandra doesn't even like children and we are too old to do this."

I squinted my eyes at him as the sun seemed to change its positioning in the sky. My heart felt like it had stopped. Were they wanting to abort it, I wondered.

"Perhaps that's something that you both should have thought about." I said, shaking my head. "I don't really understand what you're trying to tell me or ask me here."

My father stood up and took a step toward me, then away from me, showing his frustration.

"I can't raise a baby Liliana." My father said. "My lifestyle is far too dangerous."

"We're too old to raise children." Alejandra jumped in. "We don't have the time. You've seen the apartment, would you want your brother or sister growing up there."

"It's not like you don't have the money." I replied quietly. "You could move. You could change your lifestyle."

My father shook his head as he stared at me regretfully. I sighed as I put my hands on my stomach, trying to cover my baby's ears as if it made a difference as it moved around in my womb.

"Are you asking me for my approval to have an abortion?" I asked my father angrily. "I am not okay with it, if that is what you're telling me. I know it's your decision but I think you should reconsider."

"Us either! We are totally against abortions." My father exclaimed clasping his hands together and smiling. "I would never even suggest that and I realize that we made this baby, so now we have to live with what has happened."

I shook my head as I stared at him, completely dumbfounded by our conversation.

"I don't get it. What are you trying to say then?" I asked. "I feel like I am completely lost here, Papi."

"Well Liliana." My father replied. "We're thinking of signing over our rights to the child."

His eyebrows raised as he talked to me as if he was waiting for my reaction.

"Do you mean adoption?" I asked hesitantly, cringing as I said each word. "Okay, that's great then. I feel so relieved."

I stopped abruptly, realizing that there was still more my father had to say.

"I knew that you would feel that way." My father immediately said. "I also knew that you wouldn't want your little sister to be raised by strangers."

I held up my hand, stopping my father.

"You're having a girl?" I asked.

I was in shock, wondering how they already knew what they were having, Alejandra didn't even look pregnant.

"Wait, what are you suggesting?" I suddenly asked as I put two and two together. "I don't think I'm following here."

"You're such a great mother." Alejandra said. "The way you talked about your boys while you were visiting us. How you missed them."

"We just thought that maybe you and Antonio..." My father started off.

He paused and looked at Alejandra for approval.

"Would consider adopting her." My father finished off.

"Then we would still be able to see her." Alejandra said. "She would just know you as her mother and we'd never tell her otherwise."

My mouth dropped open.

"We would be the grandparents." Alejandra said. "We could come and visit. She could grow up with brothers and not as an only child, or worse if she's adopted by the wrong family."

I sat back against the bench, a million things going through my mind as I sat staring at them. My hands started to sweat as I tried to figure out what question or what to say to them next. I glanced over at Antonio who sat across the yard with his family members. Our eyes met for a moment and I was sure that he could see the confusion in my expression.

"Papi, hold on." I said, holding my hand up and sighing as I looked at him.

I put my hand on my chest to calm myself down, but could feel my heart pounding away as I tried to carefully pick out the next words to say to him.

"First, don't you think that this is something that you should have chosen to discuss with both Antonio and me together?" I asked.

"But you can convince him." My father cut in. "I know he will be against it, but this is your sister that you need to think about."

I held my hand up and shook it at him.

"No!" I said, angrily. "Papi, this is not okay. You've had your turn to talk, now give mè mine. How could you two even think about being together sexually if you don't want to be parents?"

I sighed as I stared at both of them.

"How could you not be prepared for this to happen?" I asked, shaking my head and turned to Alejandra.

"What if my father leaves you?" I asked. "I don't mean to sound harsh and I'm not saying that he'll do it, but if he leaves you, then what?"

I stared deep into her lifeless eyes. I couldn't help it; I had no pity for either of them.

"Then how will you see your baby?" I asked her specifically. "How will you watch it grow up? Do you think that you'll come here without him?"

I shook my head and put my hand on my own stomach.

"I don't know how you think that I can do this." I said lightly. "I have the twins, I'm about to have another little boy. How could you possibly think that I would be able to manage with another child?"

"We'll pay for an extra nanny." My father immediately said.

I shook my head sadly.

"Liliana, you'll have all boys, wouldn't you like to have a girl?" Alejandra asked.

I sighed and stared at her.

"How far along are you?" I asked.

"Seven months." She immediately responded.

My mouth dropped open. I couldn't even tell that she was pregnant. When I was at my father's house, I had seen her wearing sexy lingerie as she walked around the house. I could even remember the time that I had seen her and my father making love and I would never have guessed in a million years that she was pregnant, either from her appearance or from the things that she was doing with him.

"Oh my goodness." I managed to say, feeling as I was about to cry as I looked down at my protruding stomach. "I can't even tell that you are pregnant."

She stood up and held her hands above and below her stomach, revealing a tiny bump. I felt slightly jealous and didn't know what to say. I looked like a whale and she looked like she had eaten a cheeseburger perhaps, her size was just ridiculous.

"We don't have much time to sort this out." My father said convincingly. "The baby might be here sooner than expected."

Alejandra nodded her head as she stared at me.

"I didn't think that I could ever get pregnant." Alejandra said. "My ex-husband and I tried for years and he left me when he found out that I was not fertile."

She laughed lightly.

"I guess I was fertile after all.

I shook my head again.

"Wouldn't that be more reason for you to want to keep this baby now?" I asked.

She shook her head at me.

"I don't want to have a baby and not be married." Alejandra said. "Besides I'm forty three years old. I don't even know how this is possible."

I looked at my father as his face began to sweat from the heat.

"Why don't you marry her Papi?" I asked. "Then you could raise the baby together."

"No." Alejandra said, putting her hand over mine. "I don't want to. I've been married before and I'm not going to do it again."

I felt confused as I stared at her.

"Even with the baby coming?" I asked, baffled and confused.

"Especially with the baby coming." She said.

I didn't know what to say in response.

"Papi, I've been taking high school classes online." I said. "I've just been so busy, I don't know what to tell you right now."

My voice shook with every word. My right hand hadn't left my stomach. The truth was that I really wanted a girl and felt like this could be a great opportunity.

"Are you sure that it's my father's baby?" I asked Alejandra quietly.

"One hundred percent." She immediately responded, sounding slightly upset.

"Liliana, I don't mean to sound pushy, but if you don't do this for us, the baby will go to someone else." My father said. "Having a baby of our own is not an option."

Alejandra nodded.

"I don't want that." My father muttered. "Neither does Alejandra. We both want you to take her into your home and make her part of your family."

I shook my head as I sat in front of them. I didn't know what to do or say. I wanted to walk right across the yard and pull Antonio from his meeting and at the same time, I knew how strongly his relatives resented my father and I didn't want to create any more problems for him.

"I don't know." I said after a few moments. "I need some time to think about this and I need to talk it over with Antonio. Give me at least a week."

My father and Alejandra looked disappointed, but nodded their heads in agreement.

"That's totally understandable." My father said.

They both stood up and I walked them back to their car in silence, kissing them each on the cheek as they climbed in. I stood watching the car as they left, the maids immediately coming to me as I walked back into the house, noticing that something was wrong. I said nothing to any of them, silently passing by and going into the living room. I sprawled my body across the couch, feeling as if every inch of my body had just died. Sure I would discuss my father's idea with Antonio, but neither of us was prepared for what happened next.

Chapter Seventeen

The following evening the telephone rang during dinner and Antonio went to answer it. He came back and let me know that my father wanted to let us know that Alejandra had already had the baby and wanted us to come to Venezuela immediately. Alejandra had gone into labor on the airplane during the flight back home and had the baby in the middle of the airport with help from paramedics that were rushed to the scene. It hadn't been a good labor and my father was worried about them both. Neither Antonio nor I knew what to think, we didn't think the baby would survive because my father told Antonio that she was having trouble breathing and rushed separately to the hospital.

We decided to fly to Venezuela, just the two of us and I immediately called both Elena and both she and Blanca rushed over to stay with the twins while we were gone. Antonio called the airlines while I packed our bags and managed to find us a flight that would be leaving four hours later. He rushed downstairs to have the maids arrange for dinner while I rushed around, trying to think of anything that I might have forgotten. Elena quietly entered the room and hugged me, pulling back and staring me straight in the eye.

"Maybe you shouldn't be flying either." Elena said quietly, looking down at my stomach.

I shook my head.

"I'll be fine." I muttered as I gathered items for my bag and Elena followed me around the room.

I turned and glanced at her and we both smiled. She took the duffel bag from me and we quickly went downstairs and joined Antonio and his mother who were already sitting down eating dinner.

"Sorry, I was just throwing a few items in the bag that I had forgotten." I said.

"Did you pack anything for the baby, just in case she makes it?" Antonio asked. "Do you think she'll need a car seat or anything?"

I shrugged my shoulders as I cut a piece of steak in quarters.

"I guess we could always buy one." I replied lightly, before taking a bite of my food.

"You two aren't really considering this?" Elena asked after nearly spitting the food out of her mouth. "What are you thinking? Are you really going to bring the baby home?"

"I don't know, I don't know." Antonio replied. "It's just an option, anyway we don't know if the baby is going to make it, so let's just keep her in our prayers for now and we'll see what happens later."

"Antonio." Blanca started off. "I don't know how I feel about this. To love someone else's child as if it was your own."

"People do it all the time." Antonio replied. "It's not the baby's fault, why should she suffer."

"I don't think she should suffer." Blanca said. "She's just a baby. Why would I think that? I'm just saying that it would be difficult. I know how badly you both want a girl; I just don't know if this is the right way to go about it."

I let out a long sigh. She knew as well as I did that I was done. I had already told nearly everyone in the family that I didn't want to spend another day in my life pregnant after I had the baby. My goal was to go to school for accounting and to show Antonio and the rest of the family how to really work their money.

"Lily, it's just that you have so much on your plate already." Elena said quietly, as she leaned over toward me. "You have your own baby coming, how would you give both babies the attention that they need?"

"Well I didn't really have the chance to try with the twins." I replied. "I'm thinking that I can do it now. Anyhow my father said that he would pay for an extra nanny and that would be a big help for all the children."

Antonio slammed down his fist on the table angrily, his entire expression changing.

"No." He looked directly at me as he spoke. "If we decide to do this, we take on full responsibility. I want nothing from him. I don't have any respect for a man that would walk out on his child."

"Antonio." I said. "He's just trying to be helpful. He still wants to be part of this."

"I don't need help Lily." Antonio said. "Look at all this."

He motioned around the room.

"Do you think that I need help from anyone?" Antonio asked.

I silently looked down at the table. Antonio shook his head.

"I especially don't need or want any help from him." Antonio said. "I don't need that being the topic of anyone's conversations, can you imagine what they would say as it is."

Blanca nodded in agreement.

"I agree." Blanca said. "Let him play the role of grandfather, just as we do. You don't want the child to get confused. If you are going to do this, I realize that he's your father Lily, but I think that he should cut down on his visits."

She hesitated looking down at her food and then back up at me.

"What if you agree to it and they change their minds?" She asked.

"If I do agree to take her, I could never give her back." I said quietly. "They know that."

"Did you discuss that with them?" Elena asked.

"No, but I'm sure they realize that." I responded, glancing over at Antonio for approval.

"What makes you so sure?" Blanca asked.

I said nothing. Antonio backed away from the table and took his plate to the kitchen.

"What's gotten into him?" Elena asked.

I shrugged my shoulders silently. We had both wanted a girl and although we never admitted it to each other, I knew we were both slightly disappointed when my doctor told us that we were having another boy. I let out a sigh and stood up, following Antonio quietly into the kitchen. I grabbed his right arm. He glanced over at me and wrapped his arm around my waist, pulling me close to him.

"Aye Lily." He said. "What are we doing? What are we thinking about getting ourselves into?"

Neither of us said anything as we stood silently for a moment.

Elena burst into the room seconds later.

"I'm sorry Liliana." Elena exclaimed. "It's your father."

Elena had tears in her eyes as she held out the phone to me. I was confused. I hadn't even heard the telephone ring.

"Papi." I said into the telephone. "What is it?"

I frantically looked at Antonio. All that I could hear on the receiver was crying.

"Papi." I said again. "Que paso?"

There was more crying and my heart skipped a beat as my father began to stutter as he tried to get the words out. I couldn't understand a thing that he was saying.

"Papi, we're coming. Okay?" I blurted out, handing Antonio the phone and pulling him by the hand at the same time. "We have to get out of here."

Antonio held the phone to his ear momentarily and heard my father's stuttering mixed with sobbing.

"Senor, que paso?" Antonio asked firmly.

I could hear the echo of my father trying to talk again as we walked to the doorway. Antonio stopped dead in his tracks and I heard the phone go dead.

"What happened?" I asked. "Did you understand him?"

"I think he said that she didn't make it." Antonio replied.

"Oh my goodness." I said, gasping and turning to look at Elena as if it was her fault. "We have to go. I have to be there for them. They're probably so upset with me right now."

Elena and Blanca nodded their heads and hugged Antonio quickly as we walked out of the front door. Antonio decided we would drive ourselves to the airport, after calling Gilbert and finding out that he was at least half an hour away. Tears began to form in my eyes. I felt devastated. I had taken the idea of having a daughter and run with it in my mind. I was ready to take my father and Alejandra's little girl and love her as my own. Antonio put his hand on my thigh as we drove to the airport, without saying a word for at least five minutes.

"I know how you feel Lily." He said. "I was feeling the same way. I felt kind of excited that we would have a new little boy and a little girl in the house. It would have been nice to see some pink clothes instead of blue ones scattered throughout the house."

He smiled as he glanced at me quickly in the car. I smirked, attempting to smile.

"Oh Antonio." I said. "I can't even imagine how Alejandra feels. Oh my goodness. I really can't imagine."

Antonio rubbed my thigh to make me feel better as we drove. The airport seemed so far away, waiting for the plane after we arrived seemed to take even longer. As we sat silently in the airport terminal I looked down at the floor.

"Antonio, we forgot to bring the clothes!" I suddenly exclaimed.

Antonio smiled lightly and rubbed the back of my neck.

"It's okay, we're not going to be there long." He said.

I felt my heart sink as I contemplated his words. I sighed and leaned on his shoulder. I glanced around at the people at the airport. Everyone looked too busy with whatever they were doing to notice us, or the sadness on our faces. Antonio fidgeted his leg nervously as we waited for the stewardess to announce our flight. Finally after what felt like hours our flight was called and we quickly boarded the airplane. It seemed like it took less time for our flight to land in Venezuela, than it did for us to get to the airport from our house in Colombia.

"How will we know what hospital they're at?" I asked, my voice shaking as I spoke.

Antonio looked at me and smiled.

"There's only one close to the airport." He said.

I shook my head. From what I had seen in the time I was in Venezuela, I definitely didn't want to walk anywhere. Antonio reluctantly led me over to a row of taxi cabs, hesitating as he looked down at his phone.

No Turning Back

"Ordinarily I'd have a car waiting outside to pick us up." He said, shaking his head as he stared at the row of cabs.

"This is not one of those times!" I exclaimed and led him to a taxi. "We're already so late getting here."

Antonio and I grimaced as we climbed into the cab. The driver looked sketchy and although the cab was the cleanest of the cabs sitting outside, it still looked like it was dirty. Antonio spat out the name of the hospital and the taxi cab driver started driving. I exhaled as I stared out at the streets. It was late at night and it looked dangerous outside. Groups of people were gathered on street corners. Luckily the cab pulled up at the hospital within minutes and we jumped, Antonio quickly turning to pay him. I grabbed Antonio's hand and when he was done we walked toward the entrance.

"Antonio my hands are shaking." I said quietly. "I don't think I've ever been so nervous in my life. I don't have any idea what I'm going to say to them."

Antonio smiled coyly and we both let out a chuckle. I knew we were both thinking of how nervous I was when I delivered the twins. When we walked into the hospital, one of the nurses immediately brought over a wheel chair and motioned for me to get in. I smiled.

"No, it's not me." I said, smiling.

I knew she had my best intentions at heart.

"Yet." Antonio said.

A second nurse came over and stood at a distance as she watched us. I smiled lightly at them. Both nurses seemed confused. Neither seemed to understand English.

"Tell her we're looking for Alejandra?" I said to Antonio.

Antonio quickly translated for me, and the second nurse stepped forward and asked him a question.

"What's her last name?" Antonio turned and asked me.

I shrugged my shoulders.

"Déjame ver." Antonio said to the nurses, holding up his finger as he dialed out on the cell phone.

He didn't get an answer and shook his head. He turned to me as if to ask what to do and then turned back quickly to the nurses and gave them my father's name.

"Oh, claro que si." A nurse asked, shaking her head as she gave Antonio a sign in sheet. "¿Por qué no me lo dijiste antes?"

One of the other nurses at a table nearby shook her head and walked away with tears in her eyes. I felt my own eyes begin to water up as well. I imagined that the nurse had heard my father's crying as he sobbed into Alejandra's shoulder about the death of their little girl. A little girl that they had never wanted until now. I didn't know how I was going to be able to deal with my father's crying, but was determined not to point out the fact that he was going to give her up for adoption anyhow. My father was a strong man and frankly I was shocked that he was acting like this, I felt like it was totally unexpected.

Another nurse signaled for us to follow her and began to lead us down the hall and up an elevator to the maternity ward. A security officer buzzed her in before she could enter the hallway there. Rather than to lead us into one of the rooms, where mothers were, and the nurse continued walking, seemingly past all of the mother's rooms and to a room where the babies were kept. She turned to us and instructed us both to wash our hands from our elbows down.

I glanced at Antonio in shock. I didn't know what was happening, but she motioned to a room down the hall by itself and made it seem like we were going in there. I didn't know what to do. I didn't want to tell her that I had no desire to see the baby. I didn't know if I could handle seeing a dead little body. Antonio's eyes appeared calm and he stepped to the sink to begin to lather up.

"Antonio, tell her I want to see my father, just my father and Alejandra." I said.

Antonio turned to her and quickly relayed the message. She nodded her head as if she understood but handed both of us hospital gowns, hairnets and gloves, instructing us once again to wash our hands and arms. My heart pounded fiercely from within my chest. Were Alejandra and my father still in the room with the dead baby?

After we were done getting suited up, she lead us past all the newborn babies and down a hallway with separate rooms with babies in them. She finally stopped at one of the rooms and opened the door. Antonio and I both looked at her in shock as she motioned for us to enter, shutting the door behind her. A second later, my father jumped up from a chair and rushed over to me and held me tightly.

"Papi, what's going on?" I asked. "Where is Alejandra?"

My father stared at me in shock for a moment and then very slowly said.

"She didn't make it. She lost too much blood." He lowered his head further and further as he talked. "They couldn't save her. They didn't even try."

"Oh my goodness, Papi." I said hugging him tightly. "I'm so sorry."

From the corner of my eye, I watched as Antonio walked across the room and laid his hands across the top of an incubator. I slowly pulled back from my father and walked to Antonio's side, putting my hand on the clear plastic that covered the side of it. Inside, I saw the smallest baby, I had ever seen in my life. She had to be just a little bigger than Antonio's hand, and she stretched out her tiny head as if she knew we were watching her. Tiny tubes were affixed to her mouth and her skin was red and looked like it would break with the slightest touch. In spite of all of this, her tiny stomach moved up and down as she inhaled an exhaled, I was in awe, feeling like my heart had just melted awe. I became lost in the sound of the monitors beeping, indicating the baby's tiny heart was functioning. She wore a tiny pink hat, socks, and a diaper, folded over to leave her belly uncovered and I couldn't help but think that she was the most beautiful little thing that I had ever seen.

"Before Alejandra died, she saw her." My father said, his voice shaking with every word, as he stepped over to join us. "She named her Esperanza."

His voice broke and he momentarily stopped talking.

"It means Hope." He said to me, not being able to hold back his tears back any longer.

Chapter Eighteen

I didn't need to ask Antonio what he wanted to do. Each of us made up our mind to love the angel Alejandra had left behind, the moment we met her. We must have stood in the room with my father for twenty minutes without saying a word. The noise from the heart beat monitor penetrated our hearts and minds as we stood waiting to hear each beat. A nurse came into the room minutes later to take Esperanza's vitals. We both stepped forward, as if we were worried that she would somehow break this tiny little girl that opened her eyes to stare back at us momentarily. The nurse smiled lightly at us as she studied our intense gazes and left the room without saying a word.

"Do they think she'll make it?" I finally asked my father.

He shrugged his shoulders and looked away.

"I can't help it, but if I had a choice of who was going to make it, this would not have been my choice." My father said nonchalantly.

My mouth dropped open.

"Papi." I started to say.

Antonio put his hand on my arm, to quiet me. I knew what my father said was wrong, but I also knew how hurt he must feel. I looked down, feeling as if my father's words had slit a hole in my heart. My father excused himself and did not return the rest of the night. Antonio and I stood side by side for hours, watching this little angel, eventually the nurses bringing chairs into the room and trying their best to make us more comfortable.

The next day when my father came back to the hospital, he made it known that he was only coming back to sign over any necessary paperwork to make the adoption final and rushed the social worker who was assigned to us through the paperwork to make sure that he didn't have to come back to see the baby again. I tried not to be mad as he left the hospital, stating for the fifth time that he just couldn't bear being in the same hospital Alejandra had died in and stating that he would come to visit when we arrived back at home. I cried for hours, feeling like my father had no love in his heart for the little angel Alejandra had left behind.

Blanca, the twins and Elena came to join me in Venezuela the following week and Antonio returned home. He decided that he would fly back and forth between the two countries each weekend. Everyone fell in love with Esperanza and it was evident that she could feel our love, as her health slowly began to increase. Soon we were able to hold her, and she was able to open her eyes for longer periods of time, looking around the room and staring at everyone, as if she knew who we all were. Even though she was getting better and the breathing tubes were removed from her mouth, we were not allowed to take her back home to Colombia just yet. The doctors were determined to continue to monitor her, just to make sure she didn't have any rough turns.

Antonio and Elena began to become worried that we would not make it home before my due date, I was due in two weeks and hadn't had followed up with a doctor on the baby's status, regardless of the fact that we were locked up in a hospital full of doctors. A week before I was ready to deliver, the doctor released Esperanza from the hospital's care. Antonio and I decided that it would be too dangerous for either the baby or my health to fly back to Colombia, though Elena and Blanca were insistent that we get back to Colombia before the baby was born, to avoid it being born a citizen of Venezuela. Antonio decided that we would drive home and as luck would have it, I went into labor just as we approached the first hospital over the Colombian border.

The hospital was beautiful. If it wasn't nearly seven miles away from our house, I would insist that we always come here. After Sebastian was born, I lay in my bed recovering and stared out a huge bay window as Antonio and Sebastian slept. Although I could not smell the sea water, I felt as if the ocean was beckoning me in the distance from my hospital bed and couldn't believe that despite the town's beauty, Antonio and rest of the family wanted to get back home. How I would love to stay here, perhaps even move here, so I could enjoy this view for the rest of my life.

While the town appeared to be beautiful, it was apparent that the people were not, personality wise. I would have to say that this was true for everyone, nurses and doctors alike, that I came into contact with at the hospital. The nurses eyed Antonio and the rest of the family when they came to visit as if they resented them and in some ways I got the odd feeling that they couldn't wait for us to leave. After a while, in spite of the gorgeous view, it felt odd and I began to feel uncomfortable, counting the minutes until we were released to go home. When we got back to our house, I was never so thankful to be there. The drive had been such a long one, it was nice to finally spread out and relax away from each other.

No Turning Back

Although my father signed over the guardianship for Esperanza, it took until two months after we came home for everything to be finalized. I would have thought that during this time, my father would be a frequent visitor at our house, but as the months flew by and my father didn't visit us once. I became irritated that my father hadn't called or come to check on Esperanza. So much so that I decided to take it upon myself to call him update him on her health on a regular basis. By the time she was six months old, she was able to breathe on her own without any help from respirators, which I had been using with her when she went to sleep at night, per the doctor's instructions. Despite her growth, when she sat alongside of Sebastian, who was four months old, he seemed like a giant compared to her. As I watched the two of them growing up together, I wondered if she would always be that much smaller than Sebastian.

Antonio and I were in love with her. She was one of the best things that happened to us. Despite her size, she smiled, rolled over, sat up and held her bottle long before Sebastian did. I loved her just as much as I did any of the boys and I knew that Antonio felt the same way because he showed me that he did. He showed her off to his family as if she was his own blood and because of this, his family became fascinated with her. She was the baby girl that we would never have, regardless of this, I felt like my father should be more a part of this.

"Papi." I said one day on a phone call. "Why haven't you come to see Esperanza? I thought that you were going to be there for her as a grandfather like we discussed when Alejandra was alive. What would she think if she knew you hadn't been following through with her wishes?"

"You're right mina." My father said. "I'm going to come to visit soon."

"You better." I responded, without smiling. "Esperanza is getting so big. You won't even recognize her when you see her."

I laughed lightly into the phone, to lighten the conversation, but my father remained quiet. Whenever I mentioned anything about Esperanza, he didn't have a response, but if I avoided talking about her, he would talk for hours. I could tell from the sound of his voice, that he wasn't planning on coming to see Esperanza anytime soon. I didn't get it and it hurt me. I felt like he was betraying her as a father, my uncle had betrayed me, when I thought that he was my father.

After hanging up the phone with him, I walked slowly outside to catch up with Elena, who had come for a visit. She lay across a pool chair, magazine in hand. I didn't take the life we lived for granted, I was well aware that there were other people in the world who didn't get to lounge around in pool chairs all day and in some ways regretted the fact that my children would never know anything other than this lush lifestyle that we lived. I plopped down on the chair beside her without saying a word.

"What's wrong?" Elena immediately asked.

I shook my head.

"Don't lie to me!" Elena exclaimed. "You were just talking with your father weren't you? We've been through this. There is nothing you can do to change his relationship with Esperanza."

I looked over at her and did my best to smile, letting out a small sigh, and glancing up at the house.

"I know, but I've grown so close to Esperanza and she's not even my child." I said shaking my head. "I just don't get it. I wish my dad would come to visit her. A phone call from him from time to time would even be nice."

Elena glanced away and I knew she was tired of hearing me complain about my father's feelings toward Esperanza, but I went on.

"I always have to call him." I said. "I always have to be the one to inform him about her. Why? Why is he so cruel?"

I glanced at the poolside, where the twins and Elena's children tossed around a beach ball. The nanny sat in the water watching them as they splashed about. I waved at the twins when they glanced over at me, before turning my attention back toward Elena.

"He was so upset about never having the opportunity to be in my life, why is he passing up on the chance to be involved in hers?" I asked her. "Even if he doesn't want to be her father, he has the opportunity to come and go as he pleases and he chooses not to come. I just feel devastated, not just for her, for both of us."

Elena glanced down at her magazine, before reluctantly tossing it to the side.

"Lily, I'm sure that this has nothing to do with you." Elena said convincingly. "Stop beating yourself up about it."

"I know, but it still hurts me." I said.

"Lily, Alejandra and your father were in a serious relationship." Elena said. "Whether they admitted it or not. Can you imagine how hurt he must be? I can understand why he doesn't want to see Esperanza and I can't help but feel like he's not totally wrong in what he's doing. I mean Lily, seriously, imagine the pain that must be lingering in his heart."

I nodded.

"I know that he's upset about losing her. I get it" I said. "What I don't get is why he doesn't make up for it by spending time with Esperanza. Doesn't he understand that he has this amazing gift that was left behind for him? I mean she really is a miracle."

Elena nodded sadly.

"A gift yes, or don't hate me for saying this, but she is a reminder to him of what he lost." Elena said. "I mean look at her, who do you see more, your father or Alejandra? She doesn't look like him."

I shook my head.

"Well I just see her as a baby." I said. "She resembles both of them, I guess. I don't know. I kind of thought she looked like me."

Elena raised her eyebrows at me and held her hand up to stop me from saying anything else.

"Lily, when you had the twins..." She started off slowly. "Did you want to be around them?"

I bit my lip.

"That's not fair Elena." I said. "That's different."

Elena shook her head.

"Maybe you're right Lily, but your father is dealing with a loss." Elena said. "You have to let him deal with it his own way."

I nodded my head.

"You're right." I replied softly.

We both sat quietly for a few moments without saying anything else.

"So anyway, have you decided what degree you are going for?" Elena asked.

"Yes." I replied excitedly, sitting up in my chair. "I want to be a lawyer."

"A lawyer?" Elena exclaimed. "I thought that you wanted to be an accountant. You've got to be kidding me."

She shook her head.

"Do you know how long that's going to take?" Elena asked, her eyes widening to emphasize her words.

I nodded my head. Elena started to laugh as our eyes met. She stopped after a few moments and sat upright.

"Well okay then." Elena finally said, becoming serious. "I'm sure you won't have any trouble finding clients."

Chapter Nineteen

By the time I started planning for Esperanza's first birthday party, I had become highly irritated with my father. He was avoiding my calls and still hadn't come to visit. I didn't know what to do, and I was stressed out. I knew our lives would go on without him, but I wanted to be a part of all of my family's life. I knew one day Esperanza would figure out that she was not Antonio and my daughter and I didn't want her to be crushed when she found out that her father who she had grown up knowing as her grandfather had decided not to be a part of her life. Besides this, I was worried about my father. From what I heard, he was drinking heavily and making a number of enemies in the process.

"Promise me your coming to the party, Papi." I said as we spoke on the telephone. "I just finished my high school classes and I want to show you the diploma they mailed me."

"Of course mija." Was my father's simple reply.

I tried not to let emotion overcome me. I knew that he wouldn't be there and that he would do anything within his power to avoid seeing his baby girl and unfortunately, just as I imagined, Esperanza's party came and went without me hearing a word from my father. Weeks passed by with no word from him. Esperanza didn't know the difference of course, but I was devastated. I ran around the party offering drinks to people as if I was an employee, just to avoid thinking about my father and the heartache he was causing me. I hadn't seen my father in nearly a year and I was at the point where I almost felt like I didn't want him to be a part of my life. It was bad enough that he hadn't been a part of my life, and I couldn't understand why he didn't realize that this was his second chance.

Antonio noticed my disappointment and tried to distract me by taking us to the beach in the town that I had delivered Sebastian. I was so upset that even the smell of salt water and barbeques going all around us didn't help. We sat ocean side as I sulked about my father not even trying to contact me to let me know, that he was sorry for missing the party. As time passed, I couldn't help but worry about my father. While he never called me, he had never missed one of my phone calls. I tried to go about my life as if I wasn't worried, but the truth was, I was beginning to think that something had happened to him.

At night, I lay in bed imagining various scenarios but nothing in the world would have ever prepared me for what I would find out though a week later as we prepared for Sebastian's birthday party. First of all I was still distraught. I told myself that my father was okay, but something in my heart told me that I was wrong. Even though we had guests coming over the next afternoon, I still hadn't gotten around to taking down the decorations from Esperanza's party and I was going to be in serious trouble if the streamers were still pink the following day. Just as I stood in the dining room looking at the streamers dangling throughout the yard, Antonio called out to let me know that my father was on the line for me.

"I don't want to talk to him." I said, when Antonio tried to hand me the phone.

Antonio eyed me from across the room. I shook my head and looked away.

"Lily, he said it's important." Antonio said, walking over to me and trying to get me to take the phone.

"I'm serious Antonio." I don't want to talk to him, I said through gritted teeth.

Antonio stared at me intently. I knew he didn't want to have to get back on the line with my father and tell him that he couldn't get me on the phone. I looked away and stood up, walking out of the room.

"I'll talk to her." I heard Antonio say. "You have to give her some time."

I shook my head as I continued to walk to the kitchen, pausing when I got to the patio door. It was dark outside, yet I felt like I had to get out of the house. Just as I was about to open the door I heard Antonio come up behind me.

"Are you okay?" I heard Antonio's gruff voice say and turned toward him to look up into his dark brown eyes.

I shook my head and Antonio smiled.

"You can't make your father, be a father." He said sternly.

"I know." I said sadly. "It just kills me to know that he doesn't want to be there for Esperanza."

"I'm sure it kills him too." Antonio said. "It seems like he cared deeply for Alejandra and is probably regretful that he couldn't do more in order to save her."

I shook my head and looked away.

"Lily, you have to talk to your father." Antonio said.

"I don't have to do anything." I replied.

"Lily, don't be stubborn." Antonio exclaimed. "I would expect this behavior from anyone else, just not you."

"Why?" I asked. "Why does it matter to you?"

Antonio sighed and looked away.

"It doesn't." Antonio said rubbing my thigh as he spoke. "I just want you to be happy and I can see that you're not. I can see how much you care about the man."

I breathed heavily and looked away. It was a beautiful night. The crescent shaped moon bared it's reflection in our swimming pool.

"Antonio, I just can't bring myself to talk to him." I said. "He let me down. I'm tired of being let down! He promised that he would make it for her party. He's promised me over and over again that he would be there for Esperanza and for me and he hasn't been."

"I know Lilly, I know." Antonio replied, stroking my hair as he spoke. "Maybe when he spoke with you, he thought that he could handle seeing her and then realized later that he couldn't."

I closed my eyes in frustration.

"Why is it that you don't back me on this, Antonio?" I asked.

Antonio widened his eyes and moved in closer to me.

"I do, you know that I do." Antonio replied. "You are everything to me. I just want you to be happy. Don't you get it?"

Antonio looked away.

"I know how much having your father in your life means to you." Antonio said, putting his hand to his chest. "If you think that I'm on your father's side, you're crazy. The only reason that I'm civil with that man is because of you."

I smiled slightly. I knew that I was wrong for doubting him.

"Lilly, you have to talk to him." Antonio said. "It's not going to help you to avoid him. Ask him what happened, tell him how upset you are and how, him not showing up for Esperanza's party made you feel."

I nodded my head. I knew I had to talk to my father eventually.

"Listen, I love you Lilly," Antonio said. "Your happiness means everything to me."

I nodded again, and he reached over and pulled my chin towards his, pausing briefly before moving in and kissing me passionately. Within seconds we were outside, lying in the grass and Antonio was stripping off my clothes. I stared at the stars in the sky as he slipped his manhood inside of me and leaned my head back as far as it would go, letting out a loud moan as he flipped me over on top of him. As I began to move my body back and forth I glanced up at the moon. I felt like an animal and my inner beast became more and more prevalent. I leaned forward and kissed his neck, before opening my mouth and biting into it. Antonio moaned in pain and flipped me back over against the grass, moving quickly and finally finishing off.

"Lilly, what's gotten into you?" He asked, laughing as he pulled away and lay down beside me in the grass. "Ever since you came back from visiting your father, you haven't been the same."

I didn't say anything; I just smiled and looked over at him as he rubbed his hand against his neck in pain.

"I better go call my dad now." I said, standing up quickly, putting my panties and skirt back on.

I raced across the yard quickly, laughing as I stared back at Antonio who laid watching me in disbelief. I quickly walked back into the house shutting the patio door behind me. I smiled at one of the maids who stood in the kitchen, pretending as though she was cleaning the sparkling countertops. I knew that she had been watching us and at the moment I didn't care. Right now the only thing that I cared about was calling my father and finding out what his sorry excuse was for not attending Esperanza's party. I couldn't help this sudden rush of anger that I was feeling, I was going to call my father and let him know exactly how I felt. My father had never seen this side of me and he was going to be thrown off guard, I thought to myself as I grabbed my cell phone and dialed my father's number.

Chapter Twenty

"Papi," I said into the phone the moment my father answered.

I sat down on the sofa, one hand holding the phone to my ear and the other holding on to the arm of the armchair, as if that would keep me from losing my cool. I sat up straight, ready to tear him apart, my buttocks at the edge of the sofa, as if I was about to jump up and attack.

"Liliana." My father said softly, his voice filled with pain.

"How could you miss Esperanza's party?" I asked. "You promised me that you would be there!

"I know." My father said slowly. "I know and I'm sorry."

I breathed in deeply as I held the phone to my ear. This wasn't fair. I was expecting more of a fight.

"I want to know a reason." I replied. "I want you to tell me why you haven't been there for her. I want to know why you suddenly don't want to be there for me."

My father moaned painfully into the phone.

"I want to be there for both of you Liliana." My father said. "I do more than anything in this world, but it's too late for me now."

No Turning Back

I held onto the arm of the sofa tighter as my shoulders lowered and I leaned back to rest my back against the sofa.

"Well then tell me Papi," I said. "Why is it that you're not? Why is it that it's too late?"

Tears began to fall from my face as I glanced up to see Antonio standing in the doorway watching me. My father paused and Antonio came to sit down next to me. He took the phone from me and hit the speaker button, handing me tissues and putting his arm around me, pulling me close to him.

"Listen Liliana." My father said. "I want you to know that I love you, do you hear me? I love you so much."

I nodded my head without saying anything for a moment.

"Then why are you avoiding me?" I cut in and asked. "Why are you avoiding seeing Esperanza?"

I paused, waiting for a reaction. When there was none, I leaned over so that my voice was amplified on the phone.

"Don't you understand this is your second chance?" I asked.

My father chuckled; I could hear the smile growing across his face.

"My only chance was with you Lilly." My father said, suddenly sounding sad.

My mouth fell ajar.

"What are you talking about Papi?" I asked. "Are you saying that you're not going to be there for Esperanza?"

My father remained quiet on the other line.

"You can't do that!" I exclaimed. "That's not fair to her!"

Silence. I glanced at Antonio and leaned forward.

"What about me?" I asked. "Are you saying that you're not going to see me again?"

"Yes Liliana, that's exactly what I'm saying." My father said, beginning to weep into the phone. "Listen, though, you have to let me explain."

I leaned forward to hang up the phone but Antonio stopped me. He grabbed my hand and shook his head, motioning for me to listen to my father as he spoke.

"Lilly, you don't know how happy I was, learning that I suddenly had a daughter." My father said. "You are everything to me. You need to know that."

I rolled my eyes and glanced at Antonio. He still hadn't let go of my wrists and had a look on his face that concerned me. I wondered if he had picked up on something that my father had said that I hadn't. I glanced back at the phone as my father continued to talk.

"Listen, you are going to be well taken care of Liliana." My father said. "You know I own this building and I've never spent much of what I made, except on women from time to time."

My father paused.

"Cheap women." He seemed to spit out.

"I don't need to know that." I said, not meaning to say it loud enough, where my father would hear me.

"Yes you need to know that." My father said. "Cheap good for nothing, dirty tramps."

Whack! I heard something hit the phone and my father moaned out in pain.

"Listen Liliana," my father said. "There are other buildings, you'll find out soon enough, but the reason that I didn't come to the party was not because I didn't want to. This time there was another reason."

My father moaned in pain and suddenly I felt both confused and nervous. It had suddenly become apparent to me that something was going on in my father's apartment.

"Why is that?" I asked, leaning onto Antonio's shoulder, suddenly realizing that something was wrong.

I heard my father whimper and there were two muffled voices on the other end of the phone line.

"Papi, what's going on?" I asked, sounds of concern becoming prevalent in my voice.

"Do you remember that man that you heard say that wanted to kill you Liliana?" My father asked. "The man across the way while you were here?"

I nodded my head, glancing at Antonio.

"Yes, Papi." I said.

"Well he's here." My father said.

I froze and felt my heart drop. I knew what was coming and shook my head.

"No." I said softly.

"He broke into my apartment some time ago." My father said. "He hasn't taken anything. He just wanted to make my life miserable by endlessly torturing me. That's why I didn't come to the party. I really was going to go, I promise you."

I shook my head and glanced at Antonio, wondering why he appeared so calm.

"Papi, why didn't you call the police?" I screamed out.

"I can't Liliana." My father said. "He cut off my fingers."

I jumped up and put my hand to my face.

"No!" I exclaimed. "I'm calling the police from Antonio's phone, I'll tell them where you live and they'll take care of everything."

"No Liliana." My father screamed out. "You won't. It won't do you any good. He's one of them Liliana. Listen to me! You trust no one. Ever! Do you hear me?"

I sighed and tried to catch my breath, pushing Antonio as if to make him do something.

"Listen Liliana." My father said, sounding as if he suddenly calmed down. "It's okay. I've already told Antonio who they are and he promised me that he will take care of you and of everything else."

I glanced at Antonio in shock.

"So what are you going to do Papi?" I asked. "You're just not going to let them kill you are you?"

"Yes, Liliana I am." My father replied. "I made a deal with them and they agreed not to kill me until I talked with you one last time."

"No Papi." I screamed out, suddenly breaking out into tears. "That's not what's going to happen. I won't let it!"

"It is Liliana." My father said calmly. "That's exactly what's going to happen, but I couldn't leave this world without letting you know why I wasn't going to be there for you anymore."

My father let out a nervous sigh.

"Liliana, I love you." He said. "Remember that."

I sighed loudly as I stared at the phone. Who was I kidding? There was nothing I could do? "I love you too Papi." I said out loud.

My father grunted as if he was in pain.

"Hang up the phone." My father said loudly. "Antonio, if you're listening, hang up the phone now!"

My father began to mutter a prayer and we heard a click, Antonio glanced at me and leaned forward, but before he could reach it to end the call, three shots were fired. I jumped up, my hand to my mouth and started sobbing hysterically. Antonio came to my side and within seconds I dropped halfway to the ground, sobbing and clutching Antonio's knees to keep myself from falling forward on to the hard tile floor.

Chapter Twenty-One

By the time I thought of cancelling Sebastian's party, hours later, it was too late to make phone calls. Everything had already been arranged and Antonio's family insisted on giving him the party that he deserved. We had nearly 200 people at the house, twice as many as we did a week before for Esperanza's party, all this at a time where I wanted to be left alone. I felt like I was shaking on the inside, but sat silently as our guests arrived, watching as Antonio quickly greeted each one of them, whispering to them and them shaking their heads as they glanced over at me, as if they didn't know what to say. I was tempted to go inside the house and retreat to our room, but at the same time I felt like I would find out more information on my father and my father's death by sticking around the party.

Soon after the kids went off to enjoy a clown that Antonio had arranged for, his family came over one by one and offered me their condolences. As more time went by, they shared stories of my father, stories that I had never heard and stories that I wasn't sure I wanted to hear. As they spoke, I knew that many of them had very strong feelings against my father and were probably ecstatic that they wouldn't have to see him hanging around our house ever again, especially a few of Antonio's cousins who had not attended Esperanza's party, readily admitting that they had avoided the party, thinking that my father would be there.

"You're actually very lucky." Antonio's cousin Eduardo said as he left with his wife. "Have you spoken with your father's lawyer yet?"

I shook my head and he nodded at Antonio, before going on his way. I had no idea what Antonio's cousin was referring to and didn't have time to ask as more relatives approached us as they left the house. When the last guest came over and wanted to talk, I excused myself from the conversation, stating that I was tired and quickly left the room as I began to wonder if it was both of my parent's destinies to die at the hands of another man. I sprawled myself across the bed and without trying, fell into a deep sleep.

Days later my father's body was found, not in his apartment but in a dumpster not far from there. Antonio was told that his body was unrecognizable and that garbage collectors nearly threw it into the truck before seeing blood, relaying the information to me only because I was standing near him when he received the call. I didn't know how to feel and felt like I didn't feel sad or depressed enough in finding out this news.

A month later we received a phone call from my father's lawyer, stating that he needed us to go to Venezuela to sign paperwork, and we obliged, leaving the kids with the nanny taking off to Venezuela with both Marcus and Gilbert at our side. When we walked inside my father's apartment building, the looks that we received were intriguing to say the least as we walked in and the man who was supposed to do security for the building seemed alarmed to see us. He jumped out of his seat and walked across the lobby as if he had seen a ghost, glancing back at us as we waited for the elevator. Something about the look on his face made me feel very uncomfortable.

Marcus and Gilbert closed in on either side of Antonio and me as we entered my father's apartment and I spent the next few hours of the night going through my father's belongings. It felt weird being in the same house that my father had been killed in, but apparently whoever had been hired to come in to clean after it, had done a good job. The entire apartment was spotless, not a thing out of order. There was a loud knock at the door at almost eight o'clock at night and when Antonio went to the door, he seemed surprised.

"Who is it?" I asked.

Antonio turned back to the door and as he unlocked the locks he turned back to me.

"The police." He replied in a confused tone.

Gilbert and Marcus immediately stood up and came to the hallway where I was standing. Marcus pointed at my father's room and I went to stand inside, Marcus closed the door quietly the moment I was inside and I heard the front door open.

"We need to see "El Jefe's" daughter." An officer said out loud. "We were told that she is here."

I shivered and backed deeper into the room, wondering if this was one of the men that had killed my father.

"She's in Venezuela, yes." I heard Antonio reply. "I'm her husband. What do you want with her?"

"Can we talk inside?" I heard a different officer say.

"I prefer that we didn't." Antonio replied. "We don't know who you are and we don't know what you want."

"We have something very important to discuss." The same officer said. "We can only discuss this matter with the daughter of 'El Jefe'. I'm sure you understand."

"We're all here." I heard Marcus say to Antonio. "Nothing is going to happen."

I slowly came out of the room and stepped forward to Antonio's side.

"Okay then, let's do it." I said.

Antonio nodded at Marcus and Gilbert and the two police officers stared at me for a long time before saying anything.

"Can we come in?" One of them finally asked.

I nodded and walked to the living room without asking them to follow me. I didn't have to have good manners, they were intruding on my space. I quickly walked over to the window and drew the blinds. Something told me that the officers being there was not something that I wanted my father's neighbors to know about.

"How can I help you?" I asked as the officers entered the living room.

The police officers exchanged glances and leaned forward, speaking in a low tone as if everyone in the building could hear.

"Have you checked your father's apartment for bugs?" One of the officers asked.

I glanced at Antonio and he shook his head.

"No." I replied.

"What makes you think that you are safe here?" The other officer asked. "I would suggest you stay at a hotel rather than at the place your father was murdered at."

I glanced at the badge he was wearing on a chain around his next.

"Officer Gutierrez, what makes you think that I'm not safe here?" I asked.

The officer smiled and leaned forward.

"I'm not saying that you're not safe, but your father had a lot of enemies." Officer Gutierrez replied. "He had men coming in and out of this apartment throughout the day. How do you think, we knew you were here. Do you think that no one else knows that you are?"

Antonio flinched and walked forward immediately.

"What are you getting at Officer?" Antonio asked.

"Look, it's not safe to talk here, but I suggest you leave Venezuela immediately." The other officer said, reaching under the table, as if he was checking for bugs. "Can you come down to the station and talk with us?"

Antonio had a fire in his eyes that I hadn't seen before. I knew that he was attempting to make them realize who they were talking to.

"I don't know about that." Marcus said, stepping forward.

"Tell us what reason it is that you want us to come and we'll decide whether we are going or not." Antonio said gruffly.

"It is for her benefit." Officer Gutierrez leaned forward and said quietly, motioning to a picture frame on the wall.

The other officer walked over to it and nodded, pulling a small white object from the side of it and showing it to Antonio, the look in his eyes telling me that he was serious. I nodded.

"Okay." I said. "Let's go."

I didn't look at Antonio. I stood up and walked toward the door. I turned back to stare at the rest of them and the moment that I did, everyone followed, including the police officers. I saw Antonio grab the keys for the apartment and he turned to lock the door as the last officer stepped out into our quiet hallway. Two minutes later we stepped out of the elevator and into the lobby. The man that guarded the building, sat silently and nodded at the officers as we all left the building. Something didn't feel right. When we left the building the officer motioned for us to get in the car with him, but rather than abide by his rules, Antonio hailed a taxicab.

"We'll follow you." Antonio said assertively to the confused officer.

The officer turned to Officer Gutierrez and nodded at him as if to ask if it was okay. Officer Gutierrez shrugged and both climbed into separate squad cars. Once inside the taxi, Antonio grabbed my hand and held it firmly. I looked down at it and then at Marcus and Gilbert who looked like they had forced themselves into the car. Neither of them said anything or made eye contact. I glanced out the window as we drove down crowded streets. People turned to look at the police cars as if they had never seen one before. Thankfully, they turned away before the cab that we were in made it past them. I didn't know if they would know who we were or want to try to hurt us and I felt nervous as we drove past them. When we finally arrived at the police station, the officers ushered us in quickly and despite their efforts not to draw attention, we seemed to have everyone's attention within minutes as the three of us climbed out of the taxi and Antonio paid the driver.

Gilbert and Marcus exchanged looks with some of the people in the crowd outside the building that made even me shutter. It was obvious that many of them knew who Antonio was. I walked ahead of Antonio, trying to keep up with the officers fast pace. The moment we stepped inside the building, we heard a loud thud and turned to see a scrubby looking man who stood with his fist still resting against the door, that he had just pounded on. With his freehand he pointed to Antonio and then ran his finger across his own throat like he was cutting it in half. His solid expression made me shiver and I stepped over to Antonio's side, clinging onto Antonio's arm tightly.

The officers quickly called for backup and four other officers went outside to confront the man. Within minutes the man was walking past us in handcuffs as we waited for Officer Gutierrez outside of his office. Antonio moved us out of the way just in time for us to avoid being hit by a wad of the man's spit. I raised my lip in disgust and looked away. The reality of the situation that we were in set in and began to scare me. Moments later we were moved across the hall to the chief of police's office. Gilbert and Marcus were asked to wait outside while Antonio and I walked in and took a seat.

The chief came in with a stack of papers in his hand and gave Antonio and me a stern look as he sat down on his side of the desk. He put his hand on the stack of papers and immediately began speaking quickly in Spanish. Antonio stopped him and asked him if he could speak English, but the chief shook his head. Antonio nodded and within seconds the chief was quickly going off at the mouth. I couldn't understand a word he was saying but he looked mad. Antonio shot him back a rebuttal and for at least five minutes they went on like this. Periodically the chief pointed down at the stack of papers but whatever it was that he was saying didn't seem to faze Antonio. Finally when I was about to lose patience Antonio turned to me and paused briefly before he started talking.

"The city wants your father's apartment building." Antonio said.

I stared at him blankly for a moment before responding.

"All of that conversation and that's all that you come back with?" I asked.

Antonio shrugged.

"The rest of the conversation was just unimportant details." Antonio replied. "They don't think they should have to pay for it, but I told him that that's not how it's going to work."

I stared at him without saying a word.

"What do you think?" Antonio asked.

"Why is it any of my business?" I asked.

"You're the owner." Was Antonio's immediate reply.

I could tell that he was trying not to smile as he spoke.

"What?" Was all that I could come back with, a shiver going across my body?

Antonio quickly turned back to the chief and said something to him in Spanish. The chief nodded and walked out of the room closing the door quietly behind him. I turned to him in confusion and he leaned forward and began speaking quickly.

"Lilly," he said smiling. "Your father's apartment building is yours, we need to get to the lawyer's office and find out if there is anything else that you are entitled to. I will tell the chief that we want all the paperwork sent there."

I shook my head as I stared at him. I felt like I was in a dream. My father was dead and I was beginning to feel guilty about the excitement that was building within me.

"Antonio, what should I do?" I asked breathlessly.

Antonio stared at me momentarily and a serious expression came over him.

"We definitely need to talk to the lawyer, before we do anything." He said. "The city wants to close on this quickly. How would you feel about that?"

I couldn't speak. I was in shock.

Gilbert and Marcus ushered Antonio and I out of the police station minutes later and into a car with tinted windows waiting for us out back. Apparently the city had not been playing around when they said they wanted to close quickly, already anticipating my agreement. With one quick phone call, Antonio had everything taken care of. Although it was late, we were on the way over to the lawyer's office; all of the paperwork would be there before we arrived. I held Antonio's hand for the next ten minutes until we arrived. When we finally got out of the car and walked into the lawyer's office my heart began to pound heavily.

No Turning Back

The lawyer quickly introduced himself and greeted us, handing me a stack of papers moments after sitting down, for me to sign. I glanced at Antonio nervously as I took the paperwork from the lawyer. I couldn't believe that everything was happening so quickly. I couldn't help but wonder if this was legit.

"Liliana if you have any questions, please feel free to stop me." The lawyer said in broken English before rattling off as we went through the stack of papers, him describing each paper I was signing and what it meant.

Antonio glanced over the papers, handing them off to Marcus for further examination before handing each one to me for me to sign. By the time we went through the entire stack, it was midnight and the only thing left to do was to sit and wait for the lawyer to make several wire transfers and get all of my father's money into my own bank account back in Colombia. Several men entered the lawyer's office and were quickly ushered into a separate room across the hall, the lawyer excusing himself and crossing the hall to join them. We could see the men sit down and begin to look over the paperwork. The men all seemed to be in a deep discussion over the matter.

I sighed and glanced at Antonio. His eyes seemed to be full of just as much anxiety as my own were and I wondered why he appeared to be so anxious.

"Antonio," I whispered. "What's wrong?"

He glanced over and smiled at me.

"Nothing." Antonio said, a sudden gleam in his eyes. "I guess I'm just as nervous as you are. Your father said there were more buildings then we knew about and it seems that the city is buying all of them."

I smiled and neither of us uttered another word. The two of us faced forward and I tapped my finger nervously against my thigh. I eyed Antonio as the clock on the wall ticked ever so loudly. Its ticks seemed to echo throughout the room. Finally the door opened and a man with a pinstriped suit came in alongside the lawyer.

"Liliana." The man said.

I nodded at him.

"Congratulations." The man continued. "You are now the richest woman in South America."

More Great Books in The Liliana Series

Liliana
Book 1 of the Liliana series
by Neva Squires-Rodriguez

Boom!

That deafening sound changed Liliana's life forever. Her mother sits dead besides her, shot to death on the streets of Chicago.

Within weeks, Liliana is sent to live with a father she doesn't know in Colombia - a foreign land and filled with challenges for Liliana.

While working to pay off her father's debt, she meets the love of her life, who frees her from her father's illusory home, only to bring her into a new world of twisted surprises.

In Too Deep
Book 2 of the Liliana series
by Neva Squires-Rodriguez

Liliana Valencia begins a new chapter of her life. Now the wife of Antonio Valencia, Jr., she learns that there are certain requirements in being a member of the Valencia family– more specifically, Antonio's wife.

Just when Liliana is supposed to be experiencing the happy feelings of a new bride, she finds herself in a very difficult predicament. Her husband isn't the perfect man that she thought he was and she finds herself alone as her life shatters around her.

She becomes lost in a world of deceit and she struggles with the knowledge that her life with Antonio will never be the same.

With nowhere else to go but up, Liliana finds her hidden strength in a place that she never realized existed. But nothing in the world can prepare her for an unimaginable secret that is bestowed upon her. How will she ever learn to forgive and continue with her life?

Author Neva Squires-Rodriguez

Neva Squires-Rodriguez was born and raised in a neighborhood located on the North Side of Chicago. Mother, Wife, Expert at Multitasking... and now, Author, Neva creates electrifying stories with a twist.

Neva Squires-Rodriguez earned her Master's Degree from National University, a feat which she worked very hard to obtain and says she will work even harder to pay off.

She claims to be a typical American, full of dreams that will hopefully get her to a more comfortable lifestyle one day. She says, "God has a plan and I will follow wherever it is that He takes me."

Where to find Neva Squires-Rodriguez online

Website: http://NevaSquiresRodriguez.com
Twitter: @NevaRodriguez22
Facebook: https://www.facebook.com/pages/Neva-Squires-Rodriguez/1497271613835645
Blog: http://NevaSquiresRodriguez.com